Fierce Winds
and
Fiery Dragons

Dusky Hollows: Book 1

Fierce Winds and Fiery Dragons
Dusky Hollows: Book 1

Copyright August 19, 2015 Print Edition
Nan Sweet, Jeanette Raleigh

Also Available by Nan Sweet

Dusky Hollows Book 2: The Curse of the Invisibles
Dusky Hollows Book 3: Too Much School
Dusky Hollows Book 4: Adrift
Dusky Hollows Book 5: An Unexpected Adventure
Dusky Hollows Book 6: The Haunted House
Dusky Hollows Book 7: The Unicorn's Quest
Dusky Hollows Book 8: Cry of the Banshee

Chapter 1

Ivy sat in the third row at the edge of the classroom beside Carrie, which was fortunate as they were the best of friends and had been since first grade. She had (of course) been whispering when Mrs. Huffity called her name.

Swallowing, Ivy felt her face warm when David snickered. "Bucktooth lost her place. If she lost her teeth maybe she'd read better."

Glaring at David, she forgot to be embarrassed. She hated him. Fiercely.

"I'm sorry, Mrs. Huffity. Where should I start?" If only Mrs. Huffity asked the kids to read around the class the way Miss Fromm did. Then Ivy would never lose her place.

Mrs. Huffity had been wandering the classroom with the book in one large hand. For Mrs. Huffity was an extremely tall woman with bulk. Not that she was fat, not really. She just had a large frame and a large head with dark hair, tight curls, and round glasses that made her eyes look buggy. And now she was standing over Ivy's desk.

Ivy glanced up to see her teacher staring at her with those huge eyes as if she had a bird on her nose or something. And then Mrs. Huffity did a very strange thing. She tapped Ivy on the forehead and in a deep voice said, "It's time for you to open your eyes."

The class giggled while Ivy rubbed her forehead. Teachers never did stuff like that. Ivy was sure it was against some kind of rule. But here she was being tapped on the forehead. Her life could *not* get any worse. She wouldn't cry. Not in front of the class.

Ivy sighed and quietly asked, her voice getting a little high and squeaky, "Please, where should I start to read?"

With a finger that looked a bit like a talon, Mrs. Huffity pointed to a section about halfway down the page. Fascinated by the metallic brown and gold nail polish on Mrs. Huffity's finger, Ivy was distracted for a moment. But once Mrs. Huffity removed her finger, Ivy read quietly and clearly, trying to ignore the hurt she felt and wishing she could be anywhere but seated in this classroom.

She finished with a heart-felt sigh. Smiling, Mrs. Huffity turned to Carrie. It was strange the way her voice went from a light trilling to deep baritone. She said the strangest thing. "You will see a great change of fortune. Beware. Beware."

David mimicked in a whispering taunt, "Beware Carrie."

Her voice back to normal, Mrs. Huffity lifted an eyebrow to Carrie, "Have you lost your place as well?"

"No, Ma'am." Carrie was the only one in the class to use the word, Ma'am. But it seemed to make Mrs. Huffity happy for she smiled broadly revealing thick white teeth.

"Ah, then please continue."

It wasn't until recess when Ivy and Carrie ran out to the swings that they had time to think about what Mrs. Huffity said.

"You have to admit it's strange." Ivy said, pushing off the ground a little. Ivy was a cute girl, although she had been teased so much for her teeth, she didn't know it.

She did have longish teeth and wore glasses, both of which made her feel rather ugly, as if they made up the whole of her personhood. Her hair was honey gold, which is a fancy word for brown with sun-bleached blonde streaks and large green eyes flecked with gold. Her mother told her time and again how pretty she was, but Ivy didn't believe her.

6

Not really. She figured a mother had to say nice things to her daughter. Still Ivy *was* pretty even if she didn't see it herself. Mothers are usually right about such things.

"Maybe it's because she's new." Carrie bit her lip and pulled the edges of the swing in.

"Why do you think she said it?"

"She didn't mean anything by it. Change of fortune. What could possibly change?" Carrie laughed. They lived in a tiny town with only a few thousand people in it. She had twenty-three classmates. It wasn't as if there were any real options. Not the way Mrs. H. made it sound with her deep voice and scary words.

Ivy wasn't going to let it go. "I don't know. It sounded funny with the tone of voice she used. And she was serious." Then she rubbed her forehead. "Ever since she tapped me on the head, it feels tingly."

The bell rang then and the girls ran for the brick wall where everyone lined up. David was at the front with Joe bragging about his new laptop. Change of fortune. Carrie knew she wasn't getting a new laptop. Or phone. Or bicycle. Not any time soon anyway. Her parents had been arguing for weeks because her mom took her shopping for school clothes, and her dad thought they spent too much.

Ivy grabbed her hand and leaned in. "Look at our classroom. She's watching us."

The fifth grade classroom was on the second floor of the elementary school overlooking the playground. Carrie glanced up. The blinds were split apart where her teacher's fingers were holding them open, and Mrs. Huffity was looking down. It did seem that she was looking directly at them.

"Why do you suppose she's there?" Ivy pushed her glasses back against her nose, something she did often when she decided to take a closer look at something. She peered up at the blinds.

Mrs. Huffity suddenly dropped her hand and the blinds fell closed. As they filed into the school Carrie whispered, "We scared her away."

Ivy said, "I don't think anything scares Mrs. Huffity."

The recess teacher called for silence. Both Ivy and Carrie pressed their lips together as if they had never said a word. But they were both thinking about their strange new teacher and wondering what she meant by her words of caution to Carrie.

Chapter 2

Dinner at Carrie's house was spent in front of the television. Her mom had cooked a large frozen pizza and cut it in fourths. That's how she knew Dad wasn't going to be home for dinner again. Because if he were going to eat dinner, they'd have something like meatloaf or roast or steak or something good. Her mother didn't cook for just the two of them.

Carrie didn't ask where her father might be. Because it wasn't an answer that her mother knew, and she'd just start crying or angrily retreat to her room. Carrie learned not to ask some questions. They curled up together at opposite ends of the couch and acted like a normal family, but Carrie knew this wasn't normal. Dads didn't get angry and stay out until late and ignore their children for whole days at a time.

When her mother told her to brush her teeth and get ready for bed, Carrie saw a tear slide down her mother's cheek. She felt horrible. She didn't know what to say. So she went and changed into her nightgown, wishing she could make her dad stay home for dinner.

Carrie was in bed with the door closed all the way except for that little sliver that let the light from the hallway in. The front door opened and closed downstairs.

Her mother's voice carried up the stairs. "Where have you been? And don't say work."

Carrie cringed and drew her pillow over her head. The arguing would start now. She hated that part. Her stomach lurched, and she pulled herself down deep into the blankets as the screaming started. Of course, her father never said exactly where he was, just that he sure wasn't welcome in his own home.

She hated listening to the fighting. Hated it worse when the doors to the house started slamming. Cupboard doors and bedroom doors, bathroom doors as if somehow by throwing a door closed, her parents could get their point across.

Carrie started to cry when her dad went on about how much money her mom had spent on nail polish. She wasn't allowed to paint her fingernails yet, but her mom let her paint her toe nails for practice. While they were school shopping, she got to buy three colors with the sparkles and stickers.

Her mom bought her pink, purplish-pink, and blue. If she hadn't begged for the blue, maybe her dad wouldn't be so angry.

The yelling turned to muffled sobs and she heard her father storm up the stairs into the bedroom and then it sounded like he was throwing things around, opening drawers and emptying them.

She heard her mom say, "What are you doing?"

"We're done. Over. I want a divorce."

"We're just having an argument. You can't walk out like this," her mom said. Carrie hated hearing her mom sound like that or her dad for that matter. They were both so angry.

"How long? We haven't been happy for years. One more night and one more night and pretty soon, it's a life sentence."

Carrie knew he was packing the suitcase then. All of the drawers opening, the closet doors, her mom's frantic pleas. All of it meant that he was packing to go. He'd done it before, staying in a hotel for a night to cool off, but the way he was talking now scared Carrie, as if he really meant to leave and not come back. Wiping the tears from her face, she wanted to go to her parent's room and ask him to stay, tell him that she was sorry about the nail polish.

She started to crawl up from the nest of covers she'd buried herself in. Her mother said, "You promised forever, until death do us part."

"And you promised to love me, but I don't see a lot of love in this house, do you?" Her dad was storming by her door then, as if he knew she was awake and desperately wanted to talk to him. He stopped, just outside the door. Carrie wanted so badly to call to him, to ask him to stay, to find those words that would make everything better, but before she could call out, he was walking along the hall and down the stairs and out the door.

She spent long hours staring at the ceiling wondering if her dad would be home tomorrow night. She didn't think so.

* * *

Ivy's evening was much better than Carrie's, at least at the beginning. Her parents were both in a good mood because her dad just got a promotion and her sister, while a giant pest, wasn't being too bothersome that night. As a matter of fact, nothing extraordinary or interesting happened at all, at least not until she went to bed.

She fell asleep easily. That was when Ivy's rough night started. She kept dreaming that Mrs. Huffity was poking her in the head saying, "Open your eyes. Open your eyes." And then she dreamed that David was laughing and laughing. She followed him out to his locker. It was a dream, after all. She'd never do that in real life. He opened his locker and grabbed a binder pulling hard. A huge object fell crashing to his feet and broke.

In Ivy's dream, the little creature at David's feet was still alive, just a little, and crying piteously. And then Mrs. Huffity was suddenly standing there, and she was also crying in great huge gulping sobs. "You were supposed to watch her. You were supposed to care for her."

Even though the egg was in David's locker, Ivy believed that Mrs. Huffity was talking to her.

"I'm sorry. I'm so sorry." And she woke.

Ivy reached for her glasses and looked at the clock. Two in the morning. She rolled over, thinking about her dream and then fell asleep again.

The dream came back. She was standing at David's locker, but this time a shadowy figure, like an oily ghost was opening the locker. Again, an egg the size of Ivy's hand was in the top of the locker. When the ghost grabbed it, Ivy could see how pretty it was, with gold and green flecks that seemed to sparkle.

She called out to ask what the creature was doing, but her voice froze. It seemed that she couldn't move. Once again, David and Mrs. Huffity came and opened the locker. In this dream like the last, Mrs. Huffity cried because her baby was missing. "I told you not to let her out of your sight."

Ivy felt guilty. But what could she do? She kept telling Mrs. Huffity about the shadow and how it froze her. Mrs. Huffity, wiping tears and sniffling, patted Ivy's shoulder. "I should have told you to think happy thoughts. It's the only way to unstick yourself when they come. But if you saw the shadow that took the dragon then we can get her back."

Ivy woke again mumbling. "I don't like the shadow. It's cold. Too cold."

And just then her mother poked her head in the door. "Ivy, it's time to get up."

Groaning Ivy rolled over and pulled the covers over her head. "Just another minute, please, Mom?"

"Five minutes. That's it."

Of course, five minutes was never enough time when

a person really needed sleep. With the slow start, Ivy had to rush through breakfast and then she couldn't find her notebook, and her favorite shirt that she was planning to wear was still in the wash. She arrived at school in a horribly ruffled mood. And Carrie was absent.

Chapter 3

Across the white board Mrs. Huffity had written "Responsibility" and underlined it three times. Ivy frowned and wondered if it had something to do with the homework she lost on Monday. It was found after recess folded in half inside her English book. It was with great relief that Ivy turned it in for she was one who cared a great deal about grades.

Carrie's seat was empty and had been all day. Recess was boring. Ivy had wanted to tell Carrie about the dreams she had and how weird it all was. That was when Mrs. Huffity pulled out a cardboard box. It was one of those boxes that copy paper comes in. Lifting off the cover, she said, "We're going to learn about responsibility today."

The front row had a pretty good view of whatever it was in the box and they started oohing and aahing. "What is it?" Alison, from the front row, asked.

"It's an egg."

Ivy groaned and Barry, who sat in the seat in front turned and whispered. "Do you know what this is about?"

"No," Ivy wished she could say more. She liked Barry. A lot. One time he helped her find her glasses when she took them off to play. She thought she'd put them in her jacket. He was really cute with hair that flopped over his eyes sometimes. And he spent the whole time helping her look until they found them on the window ledge.

"Now, class, pay attention." Mrs. Huffity was giving Ivy the teacher stare, although parents had it, too. Ivy hated it because right after the stare, she turned pink, or fuchsia or some other shade of red, as she did just at that moment.

David raised his hand and Mrs. Huffity called on him. Ivy wondered why. It wasn't like David ever said anything useful or nice. Usually he was just being mean or silly when he raised his hand. She thought Mrs. Huffity should just ignore him, and then maybe he wouldn't raise his hand and say mean things.

"Yes, David?"

"Are we going to color it and go Easter egg hunting?"

One of the girls next to him said, "It's almost Halloween!"

David stuck out his tongue.

"No, no. This is a special project. You will each take care of the egg, one student will care for the egg throughout the day, take it home at night, making sure of course to keep it warm. That student will then return it the next morning. The egg should hatch sometime in the next few weeks, if you've all done your jobs correctly."

Lisa raised her hand. She sat in the back row. "Can you pass it around the class? I can't see what it looks like."

Mrs. Huffity lifted the box onto her desk and invited each row to walk by the egg in turn. Ivy was shocked to see that the shell looked just like the one in her dream, a gentle pink and cream color with sparkling golds and green threaded through it. Inside the box, the egg rested on a dark blue flannel blanket with pink colored hearts all over it.

David stopped in front and crossed his arms. "It's not even real. It's a fake egg."

"I assure you it's real." Mrs. Huffity was usually a very calm teacher, but her voice had an edge just then that gave Ivy the shivers.

"So what if it hatches before we each get a turn?" David asked.

"I'll take volunteers. The egg will only hatch when it is comfortable and safe."

Once everyone had seen the egg and was back at their desk, Mrs. Huffity took a pen and went to the giant calendar where their daily events were marked. "So, who wants to take the egg home tonight?"

Half a dozen hands went up and Mrs. Huffity slowly assigned each student to a day. "Now, Alison, you'll have the egg over the weekend. Will that be okay?"

"That will be fine Mrs. Huffity." Alison was the prettiest girl in class and always got the best grades. Ivy knew she shouldn't feel jealous, but she couldn't help it. Everyone liked Alison.

"Well, then you can opt out of two assignments from either Friday or Monday. For the rest of you, any day you've volunteered you can skip one assignment for each day."

"What? Why didn't you say so? Can I have a whole week?" David raised his hand. He threw one of his pencil erasers at the back of Gillian's head while Mrs. Huffity was turned to the calendar to write his name down.

"No, only a day for you to start. You'll have next Monday."

Ivy suddenly felt a whoosh in her stomach. What if David put the egg in his locker? What if he forgot it there and then pulled out his binder and the egg fell and broke all over the floor. It probably wasn't a real egg anyway. I mean what teacher would pass a live egg to her class? And eggs needed their mamas to keep them warm. Still, she had a queasy feeling because of her dream, and all of the parts of it that came true already.

After writing down fifteen names, no one else raised their hand. Of course, there were more than fifteen people in the class, but Ivy, for one, was afraid to be responsible for that egg, especially after her dream. Mrs. Huffity noticed. "Ivy, don't you want to volunteer for a day?"

"No, thank you." Ivy pushed her glasses up higher on her nose.

"Buck Tooth would probably accidentally sit on it anyway." Some of the other kids laughed. Mrs. Huffity gave David a yellow card for being mean, but Ivy's feelings were already hurt. They always called her that, David and Joe. It made her feel ugly and disliked.

Mrs. Huffity carried the box to Sara, who got the first turn. She gently put the box on her lap and looked down. "Can I touch it?"

"Gently, yes. There are some rules to taking care of an egg. Here Barry, pass one of these out to each student."

The handout said, "Care of your Dragon."

A few members of the class snickered and other whispers rose while Barry finished handing out the papers. By then Ivy had already read hers. The egg should be kept warm and always near someone who could keep it safe. According to the rules, the egg needed companionship. From the front of the classroom, Mrs. Huffity waved the rules, "Talk to the egg as much as possible. It will make for a chatty little dragon when she hatches."

Ivy raised her hand, curiosity taking hold. When Mrs. Huffity called on her, she said, "You keep saying her. How do you know it will be a girl?"

"It's just something I know." Mrs. Huffity said.

David snickered and said under his breath so that the kids around him could hear, "Yeah, because she made it up."

Ignoring him, Ivy read further down the page. Predators? Number five on the page mentioned creatures who thought baby dragons a tender morsel, quite delicious in fact. Gollivants, dwarves and minotaurs were considered dangerous with gollivants being the most troublesome to the young, although completely harmless to fully grown dragons.

She smiled. Mrs. Huffity was very imaginative. Ivy liked playing pretend, too. Sometimes she was a flying warrior with wings and a sword that whizzed through the air.

Or a mermaid with a fishy tail, and when she swam through the water no one was faster or better at swimming than she was. Something always got in the way of her day dreams. She'd be asked a question or told to get out her math book or someone would say her name. Ivy sighed. She wished dragons were real. That would be exciting.

The list didn't seem too bad. Anyone could talk to an egg for a day. And they could ignore the part about hatching because everyone in the class knew the thing wouldn't hatch. She would have liked to volunteer, but her dream was just close enough to reality to scare her. Even if deep down, she knew the egg wasn't real. So she sat quietly at her desk and wondered what Carrie was doing, and barely paid attention to Mrs. Huffity's warnings about the egg hatching process.

* * *

Carrie hadn't slept at all that night. Tossing and turning, when she finally padded down the stairs at five in the morning, she felt numb and exhausted. Her mom was awake, too, and sitting in the living room with a cup of coffee and a book. She was the waitress at Turner's Steakhouse and worked the morning shift on the weekends through Wednesday. It was Thursday, so she had the day off. Her eyes were red and Carrie knew she'd been crying all night, too.

"Mom, are you okay?" Carrie asked.

"I couldn't sleep. Nothing to be concerned about." Pulling the bookmark off the table, she marked her place.

"I overheard everything." Carrie didn't know how to say what she felt, how to tell her mom how much it bothered her that they fought.

"Do you want to stay home from school today?" Carrie was surprised. Her mom never let her stay home unless she was really sick. She had to be coughing and sneezing and running a temperature.

Her mom turned on the television and ordered a cartoon movie and they cuddled together under the blankets. The movie had just ended when the front door opened.

"Dad!" Carrie burrowed out of the blankets and sat up, her mother doing the same. She thought maybe if she got both of her parents doing something fun together, maybe they wouldn't be so angry, so she said, "Wanna watch a movie?"

"No. Your mom and I need to discuss something with you. Maybe we should sit at the table."

He wasn't always like that. Carrie remembered when he used to laugh and joke and watch movies with them. He was the official popcorn maker. Other kids had to settle for bag popcorn, but her father made the real kind with an air popper. He even melted real butter. But lately he was always serious and angry. They hadn't had a popcorn night for months.

"Dad, please, I don't want to talk about this now." Carrie was scared. She didn't want him to say it, didn't want the words to make his leaving real.

"We're going to have to." He crossed his arms and waited.

"She overheard our fight last night. I don't think you really have to tell her much." Her mom no longer sounded sad. She was angry. Carrie thought maybe her mom should go back to feeling sad, then maybe dad would come home.

Seeing that his family was in rebellion and wouldn't be making their way to the kitchen, her dad took the arm chair, sitting on the edge which made him look like he was going to leave again as soon as he said whatever it was he wanted to say.

"I found a place to stay. The next few days I'll be packing to move out."

Her mother was pale and looked like she wanted to yell or cry but for Carrie's sake, her parents stayed calm. Or maybe they just figured it didn't matter anymore if the other agreed.

Carrie just sat stunned. So this was what it felt like. A few of the kids in her class had single parents, and a few had divorced parents. They would talk about staying with their father or mother. Both of her parents watched to see how she would react. It seemed like they were expecting her to say something. Maybe they were too afraid they would start arguing if they spoke too much. She asked, "Dad, what days will I stay with you?"

"Honey..." Her dad looked uncomfortable and sad. "You'll be staying here with your mother."

"But kids always get visits. I should see you sometimes at least. You'll come to visit us?" Carrie clenched the fleece blanket she and her mom had been using.

"Every Saturday. You and me." His smile was fake, but then Carrie didn't think she'd ever have a real smile again, either.

Carrie looked over her shoulder to see her mother's reaction. Her mother was furious. And soon the fight began again. Before they went too far, Carrie screamed, "Can't you ever just talk to each other. You always fight." And she ran up to her room and slammed the door. Not that they would notice because they were too busy disliking each other.

Chapter 4

Barry's birthday was two days after Halloween. He came to school Monday of that week with a handful of invitations. His family lived fifteen miles out of town in a two-story farmhouse roomy enough for a fun birthday Halloween party. His mom made invitations for every student in the class, although Barry would just as soon Joe and David didn't show. He would forever be known as Barfy Barry after an unfortunate incident in the third grade.

Carrie stayed over with Ivy that Friday night. Ivy's mom agreed to be the chauffeur for Nicole and Trista who were also town kids. The party started at eight in the evening.

It was Nicole's turn with the egg. When her mom pulled up to the sidewalk, Nicole ran out with the box in one hand and a bag with a present for Barry in the other.

"What's that?" Ivy's mom opened the trunk for Nicole.

"The egg project from class. We're supposed to take

care of it." Nicole gently lowered the box to the trunk, lifting the lid to look once at the egg.

As Nicole climbed in the back, Ivy's mom gave her the parental look adding the additional insult of a raised eyebrow and said, "Ivy never mentioned an egg project."

"I didn't sign up." Ivy hoped the conversation would stop there. She didn't even tell Carrie about the strange dreams she'd had or why exactly she felt nervous about the egg. Something was bothering her about the whole thing and *she* wasn't going to be the one to accidentally kill a baby dragon.

"Honey, it's important that you participate in class activities." They were just turning onto Main Street. Ivy hoped her mom wouldn't use the whole drive to lecture her on school projects, especially in front of Nicole and Trista who were her second-best friends.

Carrie intervened with the details for Ivy's mom, "Mrs. Huffity is really cool. We're babysitting an egg and if we pick a day to watch it, we can skip turning in one assignment for that day. Two if we have the egg over the weekend. I was out that day. When I came back, I signed up."

"You chose to do all your assignments rather than

watch the egg?" Her mother had a thoughtful expression on her face. Ivy couldn't quite tell if she was pleased or wondering why. It didn't really matter. Ivy and her dad did homework together when he came home from the office, and she actually looked forward to it. He'd always make fun things out of it, like the time they raced doing times tables or the way they made a crossword puzzle together for spelling words. Carrie was with them one night and said Ivy took a lot longer doing her homework, but Ivy didn't really care much if she did.

The wind was blowing and it was twilight when the girls arrived. Three cars were already parked in the dirt near the shop while several people milled about in the front yard. Most of the parents were standing in a small group near a table set up with three large red and white juice dispensers and plates of cookies. With the wind blowing, the plastic wrap from one had already picked up and flown off the table while Barry's mother chased after it. A large cake under tin foil was set to the side. Barry and a group of boys leaned on the fence, throwing rocks into the field while two of the girls from their class sat on the steps talking.

Once the guests had arrived, Barry's father announced a scavenger hunt. The kids lined up to pick a number out of a hat. Ivy was secretly relieved that neither David nor Joe had come. Not that they would. Large signs with numbers were posted around the yard. The kids found their number, picked up a list of the scavenger hunt items and a pencil, and went to their group. Carrie drew a number four. Ivy was disappointed when she drew a seven. They moved off to their separate teams and waited for everyone to finish drawing.

Ivy's mom agreed to watch the egg. She and Barry's mother sat in lawn chairs in coats with the egg box in between them. Noticing the gleam of egg from where she waited, Ivy ran over before the hunt started and pulled the fleece blanket that was sandwiched to the side of box to cover it. "Mom, you have to keep the egg warm."

Her mother tweaked a few of her bangs. "We'll take good care of it. The game is starting."

Barry's mother laughed. "Barry's already had a turn at it. He almost forgot to take it back to school. I'm pretty sure it sat in his closet all night."

Ivy missed whatever her mom had said because the whistle for the start sounded. She ran to catch up with her group. With the night coming, they all had flashlights and moved out in every direction, along the fence line to the barn and hayloft while a few kids went to the shop. Others ranged closer to the house, looking along the tree line or in the shrubs.

Ivy found the purple ribbons. They were tied to a hook on the barn. She could hear squeals and laughter in the dark and jumped when Barry, who was on her team shouted, "I found the red rock."

No one grumbled that Barry was allowed on a team, even if the scavenger hunt was held at his home. After all, it *was* his birthday party. Barry's two older brothers, wearing creepy skeletal Halloween masks jumped out at Ivy's group as they left the barn. Ivy and Maeve screamed and jumped back, laughing.

The sun went down and a chilly wind blew across the fields. Ivy stopped her team long enough to zip up her jacket. By the time the scavenger hunt was over, Ivy was tired but happy. They lost having only found ten of the fifteen items on the list, but they'd spent much of the time giggling or running from Barry's brothers. When they returned, Ivy noticed the egg sitting by itself under the chair. The two women had moved inside, taking a plate of cookies with them.

The kids all stopped for refreshments. Ivy ignored the

cookies and moved straight toward the lawn chair. Barry followed. As she reached down to pick up the box, he said, "There's a really warm place in our laundry room where I kept it when I was outside feeding the lambs."

She looked up startled and smiled shyly, "We can take it there. Thanks."

Barry led the way to the front porch. Nicole waved her thanks when Ivy pointed to the box and the door. Ivy smiled and nodded. Inside the front door was a mud room filled with boots and sneakers. A washer and dryer sat along the wall next to the door to the kitchen. A large shelf with detergent and fabric softener, a feather duster, and light bulbs had an open spot. The box fit perfectly.

"It is warm in here," Ivy said. The dryer was running, a sound that she loved. She thought the egg would be happy here in this little room, at least for a while.

Ivy laughed to herself. Everyone would think she was crazy if they knew she was treating the egg like a living being. All of the other students joked about Mrs. Huffity's egg and her stories about baby dragons.

Once the box was tucked safely away on the shelf, Barry said, "Do you want to see my dad's saltwater aquarium? It's really cool. We have anemones, clown fish, even shrimp for cleaning the tank."

Ivy pushed a strand of hair away from her forehead nervously and adjusted her glasses, "I'd love to."

Barry liked to talk about his dad's aquarium. Whenever a class project allowed it, he picked marine mammals, sea creatures, or tides. He always picked something to do with the ocean. His father was a wheat farmer and raised cows, pigs, and lambs, but he took Barry and his mother to the coast last year. They went on a whale watching tour and everything. His dad couldn't even buy anything for the aquarium unless he drove two towns over.

The aquarium was huge, massively huge, taking up a whole wall in the living room. The mothers chatted at the kitchen table while they snacked on cookies and drank coffee. Barry's mother waved them in when Barry asked if they could go to the living room.

"I think Barry has a crush on her. Isn't it cute?" Barry's mom asked in hushed tones that both Barry and Ivy overheard.

Ivy could feel her face warming and glanced at Barry who was looking at her in horror to see if she'd heard. Then Ivy heard her mom say, "They grow up so fast."

She didn't want Barry to feel bad. He looked like he

was ready to run right out of the house. Ivy said quickly, "I wouldn't mind being friends if you want to."

"Really?"

"Yeah."

"You don't care that Joe and David call me Barfy?"

Ivy rolled her eyes and crossed her arms, "Why would I care what those two jerks think?"

A smile spread across Barry's face, "Okay, we'll be friends. Come check out the aquarium."

Barry pointed out the shrimp at the bottom and the bright fish darting through the coral. He showed her the pumps, "A proper saltwater aquarium has to have pumps so the water moves across the aquarium like the tide. The fish need something to swim against. See the anemones?"

"Wow," Ivy said in a hushed tone. His tank was larger than the ones in the pet store, larger than anything she had ever seen and it took up the whole wall. "It's so big. You've even got crustaceans." She tried out the word she'd heard from Barry's report on crabs and lobsters.

"My dad likes having it, but he did say it was a lot of work. Also, since we put it in, it will be harder to sell the house if we move."

"Are you going to move?" Ivy felt horrified. She and

Barry had just decided to be friends and now he was talking about moving.

Barrie shrugged. "The wheat prices have been down a while. It makes farming tough."

It was something Ivy heard a lot. Many of the farmers in the area had already gone out of business and moved away. The problem with Dusky Hollows was that there wasn't much to do for work. The town had the schools and a small nursing home, a pharmacy, grocery store, a few restaurants, one gas station, a building for the forestry service, and some banks. So when people wanted to look for work, it wasn't very easy to find. She knew that Barry's mom had taken a job with the post office when Mrs. Harvey retired.

They spent a few minutes watching the fish when Ivy thought she heard something. She got an eerie feeling. It was like a drop of water splashed right in the middle of her back, one that rolled down her spine leaving a strange, creepy feeling. "Did you hear that?" She whispered.

Barry was watching an angel fish swim through the coral, "Hear what?"

"It's like someone breathing with a cold. You don't hear it?" Ivy had been hearing a lot lately that no one else heard.

"No. Do you know where it's coming from?" Only one light was on in the living room casting strange shadows about the room.

Ivy pointed back to the kitchen.

Barry said, "Let's investigate."

Relieved that Barry didn't give her a funny look and ignore her, Ivy followed him into the kitchen and out onto the porch.

"Do you hear it now?" Barry asked, his voice low. He had a gleam in his eye and seemed to be enjoying the mystery.

She turned to look into the back of the little room and there detaching from the shadows was a creature with a sharp beak and rasping breath. "Tell me you see that."

Barry stared at the empty spot where Ivy pointed. "See what?"

"Hmmm..." Ivy's heart pounded while she took that first step toward the creature. She didn't want to do it. But right now the creature was closer to the egg than she was. It looked at her only once, and then the strange face turned up toward the shelf, calculating the best method of climbing to the egg.

Barry stormed onto the back of the porch sending the creature that scared Ivy skittering back. It chittered angrily at him. He almost ran right over it. He asked, "What is it? What do you see?"

Swallowing, Ivy stepped closer to Barry, trying to see figure out where the creature went and not wanting to admit that she could see something he couldn't. He would think she was crazy! That wasn't a good way to start out a friendship. Neither was lying, so she told Barry the most gentle truth she could. "I'm not sure what I saw."

Barry reached up and grabbed the egg from its perch on the shelf. "Do you want to see more of the aquarium or go back outside?"

"The aquarium...unless you think you need to return to the party." Ivy said.

When they walked back through the kitchen, Ivy's mother exclaimed, "Oh, that egg box. I promised the girls I'd look after it." She took the box from Barry and set it under the kitchen table. Ivy wondered if the creature she'd seen would just crawl right into the kitchen while her mom was oblivious to everything and steal the egg and eat it. She had heard the strange breathing all the way to the laundry room. Maybe if she stayed close, Ivy would hear it again.

They went back into the living room and watched the fish swim for a while. Ivy strained to listen for the sounds of the strange beaked creatures.

The rest of the party was uneventful, except that Ivy found a new friend. Barry turned out to like the same music and the same books, except for *The Little Princess*, but Ivy could hardly blame him for preferring *Where the Red Fern Grows*. Carrie was tolerant of his inclusion. At first Ivy worried that she might be jealous, but Carrie was worried about stuff at home and they were such good friends, Ivy knew nothing would hurt their friendship.

Chapter 5

After the Halloween party, nothing exciting happened
with the egg for a few weeks and once the dreams had faded,
Ivy stopped paying attention to whose turn it was and
whether the egg was safe. At least she tried very hard to put
the worry far from her mind. If she failed, it was only
because she couldn't get that strange creature out of her
mind.

So far, the egg had made the rounds, and usually
ended up in the box at the feet of the person whose turn it
was. Carrie was having a rough time, so Ivy tried to console
her friend, not worry about some project she didn't sign up
for anyway. And yet, that egg really bothered her.

When the school bell rang, she and Carrie were still
trying to find one of her gloves, which she was sure she'd put
in her desk. They finally found it in her backpack pocket.
Feeling sheepish, Ivy apologized to her friend.

"It's okay. Do you have to be home right away?
Maybe we can swing for a while."

"My mom works until five tonight. I can stay that long."

That was the great thing about living in town. They walked to school while the country kids had to ride the bus. Although secretly sometimes Ivy was jealous because the country kids raised lambs or calves and showed them at the fair. And they also showed up two hours late to school when it snowed because the buses couldn't drive that well in the snow, or they had early dismissal.

The girls walked out of the classroom together to see David pulling the egg out of the egg box and pushing it into the top of his locker.

"Hey, you're supposed to take that with you." Ivy put her hands on her hips and then realized she probably looked like her mother and crossed them instead, which looked like her father. She sighed heavily.

"You're so dumb. You have to turn in all the assignments. I'm doing my egg duty. *My way.*" The box didn't fit so David tucked it under his arm and left the building.

Seeing the indignation in Ivy's eyes, Carrie said, "We'll tell Mrs. Huffity tomorrow morning. David won't get a free day."

"We can't wait. Do you know where Mrs. Huffity went?" Ivy wasn't the best at paying attention and didn't quite catch what Mrs. Huffity said to the girls when they were deep in the hunt for Ivy's gloves. But she knew one thing—if that egg was left alone in the school overnight, something horrible would happen to it.

"She went to the office to talk to Mr. Joyce." Carrie thought for a moment. "David's combination is taped to the top of his desk lid. Every time he lifts it, I can see it."

The girls looked at each other and then back at David's locker. Ivy frowned, "How much trouble do you think we'll get in?"

"I don't care. I'm tired of doing what everyone tells me." Carrie's eyes had a spark of anger and Ivy knew there was no sense discussing it with her, especially since Ivy wanted to break into the locker, too.

Besides, it wasn't like they were going to take anything except the egg, which needed looking after. After writing down the combination, Carrie opened David's locker by herself, explaining, "There's no sense in both of us getting in trouble if the principal comes along. Just watch the halls."

But the halls stayed empty. With a triumphant grin, Carrie gently coaxed the egg to roll into her fingers. Now that the egg was without it's fleece-blanketed box, it looked lonely and strange.

Carrie held it in her hands and her mouth fell open, a look of awe spreading across her face. "What if it's real? I mean, I feel it in my hands and I think it's moving a little."

Ivy watched. It did seem like the little egg was trembling in Carrie's hands. Although it was so big that it probably felt the cold and was reacting. After the strange dreams she'd had and the creature she'd seen at Barry's, she knew the egg was real.

"Maybe it's cold. It's used to all those blankets. Maybe we should tuck it into our coats." Ivy touched the egg and felt a strange thrumming under her fingertips. She could hear a strange noise almost like a single flute playing a very low note, but it was also an animal sound. She looked around, "Do you here that?"

Carrie leaned closer to the egg, "I think it's coming from this. Here, you have that fleece with the pockets under your coat. You can wrap it in your winter coat and still be mostly warm."

Ivy's mother believed in layers. Sometimes Ivy took off her coat, but still wore her jacket in the school. It was purple and warm. Unzipping her coat, Ivy took the egg and tucked it inside, zipping the coat back up around it.

"Can you keep it at your house?" Carrie's room was a mess, clothes in boxes for what her mom called a downsizing. Since her dad found another place to live, they were selling the house and moving to the single apartment building in town. Really it was more like a four-plex with four apartments in the one building, but it was close to the school. Her town didn't have many apartment buildings.

Ivy thought the egg was moving again. "Yes. We'd better hurry. Someone might wonder what we're doing here." She felt guilty for stealing the egg from David's locker. She worried that everyone would know what she did if they saw the two girls in the hall.

Carrie and Ivy walked to Ivy's house from school. The weather was cold and the sky was completely gray with a single cloud that blanketed the entire sky.

While the girls walked home, Ivy tried to think of a reasonable explanation for having the egg. If she told her mom that she changed her mind, her mom might say something to one of the other parents, and it might get back to Mrs. Huffity. Carrie wanted to tell Mrs. Huffity the whole story, but knowing she'd done something wrong, Ivy wasn't eager to confess her part in it.

At Ivy's house they searched for something to keep the egg warm. Pulling an afghan throw that her great Aunt had knitted out of the closet, Ivy made a little nest. The two girls sat for while with the egg waiting for it to do something, but it didn't seem to be moving anymore. Carrie frowned, "I hope we didn't kill it when we took it out into the cold."

Thinking of the little creature dying in her dream, Ivy's face blanched, and she felt sick to her stomach, "Do you think we might have?"

Carrie shrugged. "I don't know. I hope not. I have to get home before Mom freaks. I wish I could stay with you."

Ivy secretly wanted to have the egg to herself for a while. She wanted to talk to it and see if it answered back. But Carrie's feelings would be hurt so she said, "I know. Maybe you can call me tonight after my mom gets home?"

Both girls knew that she wouldn't get to sleep over on a school night. After Carrie left, Ivy turned the lock to the door just the way her mom and dad told her to do when she was home alone. Most people in small towns didn't regularly lock their houses. But she was the only person in the house, her and the egg.

Ivy closed the door to her room and sat next to the little nest she had made with the afghan and put her hand on the egg. It rocked a little and felt surprisingly warm. "Mrs. Huffity said you were a girl dragon. I should probably give you a name."

Ivy took off her glasses and rubbed her nose. Sometimes they made her face hurt. Setting them aside, she picked up the egg, afghan and all and set it on her lap using the wall as a back rest. "Dragons are fiercesome creatures. You should have a strong name."

A rasping sound near the window startled Ivy and she jumped a little. One of the beak-faced creatures came right into the room through the wall as if the wall didn't even exist. Now that she could get a good look at it, she could see that the creature had brown tufts of fur around it's face, although the beak looked cruel. She could imagine it pecking a hole right through the egg. She knew then her dream had been true. If she and Carrie had left the egg in David's locker, the creature would have found it.

A minotaur was a man with a bull's head and a dwarf was like a little man with a thick beard who liked to mine. So that left a gollivant. Ivy pulled the egg closer lifting, her knees to protect it while the gollivant stalked across her bed on strange, furry legs sometimes going two-legged, sometimes on all four before stealthily dropping to the floor.

"Stay away from me." Ivy's mouth felt dry and she could barely get the words out. She wished she could reach the teddy bear sitting on top of the bed, but it was too far away and the gollivant was in between. Still, it would make her feel better.

The creature knew it was being talked to. With a tilt of its head, it squawked and lifted two wings as if to make itself larger. Ivy hadn't seen it fly yet, but she had no doubt that it could.

"Shoo." With the egg in her arms, Ivy lurched forward as if to attack and the creature jumped back. Another one flew through the wall, alighting on her dresser where its claws clicked as it tried to gain purchase. Giving up, it soared right over her head and landed next to her closet.

Ivy pushed herself back from the wall with her arms full. She carefully stood. The two creatures squawked and hopped and Ivy hurried to the door with a fast walk. She closed the door behind her even though the creatures seemed to move through walls.

It was a strange feeling to be frightened and alone and still be responsible for something. Funny that the word Mrs. Huffity wrote on the board regarding the egg was *responsibility*. Mrs. Huffity must have known how much trouble the egg would be. Why would she have her students care for something that important?

Mrs. Huffity said that gollivants didn't hurt humans. Ivy turned on the television to a cartoon and turned up the volume, hoping that the gallivants would be scared by the sound. She laughed aloud every time anything happened. Every light in the living room was on. At first she sat at the edge of the couch with her awkward bundle and waited for something to happen. When nothing did, she curled up on the sofa encircling the egg and relaxed.

Her mom came home first, a half hour before Dad. Chill air blasted into the house when the door opened. Ivy half expected the two creatures to be sneaking in with her mother, but nothing of the sort happened.

"Oh, turn that thing off."

Ivy hit the power button on the remote. "Sorry."

"What's going on?" Pulling off her gloves and coat, Ivy's mom opened the closet door. Ivy gasped and stifled a scream when she saw one of the gallivants crawling down the side of the door as if it were a spider the size of a dog. Her mom didn't notice anything.

"Do you have any letters from Mrs. Huffity?" Her mom shut the closet door, but the gallivant was already sitting on it's haunches in the hall staring at the egg with a hungry look.

"No." Mrs. Huffity sent letters home to be signed when one of the students got in trouble. Ivy had a letter for missing homework the first week in October, but that was the last time. Her mom had been checking her backpack ever since. Ivy still lost her papers every now and then, but most of the time she found them in the backpack pocket because her mom would tuck any homework she found in there.

"Did you and Carrie fight?"

Now Ivy was angry. "No! Why would you think that?"

"You look guilty."

Guilty. Was that how her mom always knew when Ivy was in trouble at school? Ivy thought the truth was probably better than any other excuse she could come up with. Otherwise her mom would think she lost her homework again or that she really did have a fight with Carrie. She didn't want to get her friend in trouble, so she decided only to tell her own part of the story. "It was David's turn to take care of the egg. He left it at school, so I took it."

Ivy lifted the afghan so the gold-speckled green egg was visible. The gollivant that was hunched in the hall straightened up and started to move to the wall to get closer.

Ivy immediately hid the egg again. But the creature still sniffed the air and seemed to know where it was.

"Well, honey, as long as you bring it back tomorrow morning, no harm done." Her mom laughed, "All that over an egg."

At the sound of her mom's voice, the gollivant disappeared, poof and it was gone. Ivy let out a huge sigh of relief. Sinking back into the couch Ivy realized that she was hungry. "What's for dinner?"

"Meatloaf and baked potatoes. It will be a while. Do you want a cheese stick or an apple?"

"Can I make oatmeal cookies?" Ivy asked.

Unlacing her shoes, her mom said the same variation of what she always said, "You're better off eating healthy. Someday you'll thank me for it." Her mom was still in her nurse's uniform. She had a name tag and hat and everything. As she spoke to Ivy, she unpinned the hat.

Ivy wrinkled her nose at the suggestion. "Oatmeal is healthy. Maybe we can have sweets once a week, as a compromise?"

"You had cake and ice cream at Barry's party."

"That was two weeks ago!" It was so unfair. Carrie's house was stocked with ice cream, chocolate, peanut butter cups, powdered doughnuts, and chocolate chip cookies. And the worst was that Ivy's mom had asked Carrie's mom not to give her sweets, so the only time she got anything at Carrie's was by sneaking it, which didn't happen often because Carrie got grounded the one time her father caught Ivy eating a brownie. And then he called Ivy's mother. Ivy didn't get grounded, just an excessively long lecture about fuel for the body and food for the mind.

Ivy sighed. She didn't feel thankful, but at least her mom had scared off the predators waiting for her to forget the egg.

After dinner it was Ivy's bath time. Sometimes she took showers, but she still liked baths a lot, too. As Ivy got her pajamas ready, she called out to her mother, "Mom, can eggs get wet?"

Ivy had kept the afghan and egg with her the whole time. "Let me see it."

Her mom picked up the egg, looking at it and feeling the surface. "I don't see why not. Don't you take that blanket into the bathroom. It's the only thing I have from Aunt Hilda."

"I won't."

Ivy poured her favorite princess bubble bath into the

tub and let it fill up. The egg was safely settled onto her towel. Once the tub was full, she'd step in and then put the egg in, too.

The egg half-floated and Ivy started pushing it along the bubbles playing in the suds. As her fingers played along the smooth part of the shell, the egg rocked sending ripples through the water.

For a moment Ivy was excited, but then she felt a bit of fear when she wondered if the creature inside was drowning. Of course her mom would say the egg was safe. She didn't believe it was real.

Ivy lifted the egg out of the water, holding it in her hands while it rocked back and forth. Whispering that everything would be okay, Ivy thought of when she was sick and her mom sang to her. In a low voice, she sang all of her favorite songs, but instead of calming the creature inside the egg, it just rocked harder. Finally Ivy decided that she would have to put the egg outside the water. She was afraid of drowning it, and she had to wash her hair.

She hurriedly poured a dollop of shampoo on her hand and scrubbed her head, then she dunked herself in the water and scrubbed more. Sometimes she would turn on the water and put her head under the faucet, but today she was in too much of a hurry.

Ivy pulled the stopper to drain the water. And hurriedly changed into her pajamas. The last half hour of the day she crawled into bed to read. Today she tucked the egg into the corner, making a nest so that it wouldn't fall into the crack between the bed and the wall. Reading aloud, she watched the rocking motion and wondered if the little dragon would hatch while in her care.

When her mom called out that it was bedtime, she groaned because she was right in the middle of the chapter, but she closed *The Princess and the Goblin.* One night a week she could read a half hour past bedtime, and she'd already used her night.

With the lights out, the room took on a sinister feeling, mostly because of the strange breathing that slowly seemed to fill the room. She could see bits of movement, but when she turned her head, nothing was there. Swallowing, Ivy crawled to the end of the bed and picked up the egg. Frightened noises seemed to be coming from inside.

"It's okay, I won't let them hurt you." Ivy spoke to the egg, her voice barely above a whisper.

She felt something drop onto the bed covers, jiggling the mattress and screamed. Her dad ran up the stairs and threw open the door, turning on the light. "Are you okay?"

The gollivant crawling toward Ivy stood up and turned around, looking right at her father who never even saw it. He seemed to look through it to Ivy. She said, "There's something in my room."

"You probably just had a bad dream. There's nothing here. Want me to check under the bed?"

Ivy swallowed. She did want him to check under the bed. Not that she had asked him to since she was at least eight. I mean ten years old is old enough to know that there's nothing under the bed, but this one time, there just might be. Not that anyone else could see it.

"Yes," Ivy said.

Lifting the covers from the foot of the bed, he knelt down. Ivy was afraid the gollivants might jump out and hurt him. He reached down under the bed. "Be careful, Daddy."

Her dad chuckled and then with his arm under the bed said, "Because the...fuzzy teddy bear might jump out and hurt you." He said the words loud and fast, startling Ivy. She screamed again and jumped.

"That's not funny."

"I'm sorry. I shouldn't have done that when you were already scared."

"Can I stay on the couch with you for a little while?"

She was surprised when her dad said yes. "Just this once. It's snowing so you might not have to go to school tomorrow."

"Really?" And then, with egg in hand, Ivy ran to the window to watch the giant snow flakes falling. She shivered and jumped back from the window when something came running across the yard toward the house.

More than once the creatures started crawling toward her until her dad said something or the television noise scared them and then they popped out. And her dad never even saw them.

When her parents went to bed, Ivy had no choice but to return to her room. The snow had already started sticking and from what the weather man said, it was going to be a record snowfall. It hardly ever snowed in November and never like this. That's what her dad said, anyway. Everyone online was reporting it as a freak storm.

Now she was alone and scared.

Ivy pulled the egg under the covers with her. Five creatures were surrounding her bed. One was crawling along the ceiling as if gravity meant nothing until it was directly over her head. "I won't scream. I won't." Ivy said over and over, willing the creature to go away.

Staring at the ceiling, she froze, waiting for something to happen. The gollivant was staring at her with large yellow eyes. It moved a few inches sideways, still watching her. Its eyes flickered for a moment toward the egg. Pulling the egg into her arms, Ivy glared at the gollivant. "You'll have to go through me first." She felt brave saying it, mimicking Carrie's favorite phrase when they were playing Stratego.

And she was beginning to think that maybe the creatures couldn't do anything after all. They only seemed to hover and wait, at least until the one on the ceiling dropped onto the bed and seemed to go through the covers and land directly on the egg. She felt the creature's fur on her arm. It was warm and soft, the kind of fur she would want to pet if it were attached to a cat or dog.

A tug of war began with the egg in the middle, but Ivy had a decent hold on it no matter how hard the wiry little creature pulled. Two more dropped onto the bed, one put a foot on her head trying to reach it. With sudden inspiration she pulled her body around the egg and rolled over, the creature squawking and falling off the bed.

Ivy never knew how long it lasted but she lost her fear of the creatures. They were furry and only cared about getting to the egg. They didn't use their beaks to peck at her. At some point the creatures gave up and somehow Ivy fell asleep in what was the longest night of her life. But as she slept fissures split along the egg, cracks appearing where once the side was smooth.

Chapter 6

It was still dark when Ivy opened her eyes. Her shoulders and arms ached from the battle to protect the egg. Her cheek was resting against the shell and vibrating along with the egg while a tapping sound echoed near her ear. Remembering the mess eggs made when she made cakes with her mom, Ivy decided to remove herself and the egg from the bed. No gallivants were present but she took no chances.

A night light was on in her room. Not that she needed it, but she was grateful that she could sneak around her room without turning on the light and alerting her mom that she was awake. The tapping from the egg continued.

Ivy pulled her painting shirt from the bottom of her dresser. It was her Dad's shirt and for a long time went to her knees. Now that she was older the shirt looked ragged with splotches down the front where she had spilled when she painted. A few holes were starting to show at the seems and every time she wore it, her dad threatened to throw it out.

After settling onto the floor in her bean bag chair with a bundle of blankets and the egg wrapped up in the t-shirt on top of her lap, Ivy sang to the egg very quietly. Her parents turned the heat down, so it took a minute to get warm under the pile of fleece. Realizing that the egg must be cold, she decided to draw one of the blankets up over the egg. She made a little tent for it and poked her head inside.

Tapping and rocking the egg rolled first one way and then the other. A crack split wider and it seemed for a minute that the egg would break right open, but the shell held firm. Ivy was drifting off to sleep again when she heard a squawk that startled her awake. She lifted the blanket and peeked at the egg. Shells were scattered along the t-shirt and sticking to the blanket. A pair of large eyes inside a small dragon body watched her.

"Hello?"

Ivy wondered if the dragon understood what she was saying. "Are you hungry?"

And she had a sudden sinking feeling. The egg-care and dragon instructions were in her desk in school stuffed with a hundred other papers. She had no idea what the dragon would eat or how to care for her. The dragon leapt onto her shoulder and hissed when a gollivant appeared just behind her. Ivy jumped back, hitting the wall. The dragon squeaked and tightened her claws on Ivy's shoulder, which hurt.

"Hey!" Ivy reached around to lift the dragon away, but the dragon butted Ivy's hand and loosened her grip without intervention.

Three gollivants were now surrounding her and snitching pieces of egg shell and gnawing on them happily as if they were slices of chocolate.

"You can have all of the egg shells you want. Just leave the dragon alone." Ivy said sternly, feeling very brave now that she knew they wouldn't hurt her.

The clock said seven-thirty and was about to go off. Ivy stood with a hand on the dragon's body to help her balance, and carefully shook out the towel, letting the egg shells fall to the floor while the little creatures giggled and chittered. Turning off the alarm, Ivy looked at the dragon and then her backpack. It was the only way to get the creature to Mrs. Huffity without her parents seeing the little creature, but would the dragon go willingly?

Deciding to save the backpack for later, she got dressed, pulling on her jeans and a fleece button-up shirt with pink and purple plaid. Her sneakers were downstairs by the door, but she pulled on a pair of white socks and then scratched the dragon's head. The dragon made a soft sound that Ivy decided must represent happiness, something between a purr and a trill.

Ivy stuffed one of her doll's blankets into the bottom of the backpack and carefully lowered the dragon baby into it. With a contented sigh, the dragon curled up and even allowed Ivy to zip it closed. She left a small opening for air flow. Glad to get the first problem over, she lifted the pack onto her shoulder and headed downstairs for breakfast.

Her mom and dad were both sitting at the kitchen table, Mom in her robe and slippers and Dad in suit and tie. "Up so soon?" Her dad chuckled. "We were going to let you sleep. School's canceled."

"But I have a project." Ivy thought of the warm little body in the backpack snuggling up to her shoulder.

"Everyone's going to be out today. The project can wait until tomorrow."

Ivy thought of the paper in her desk telling her about the proper feeding and safety for a dragon. Normally it was something that would interest her. At least it wasn't social studies, but somehow she managed to ignore most of what was on the paper. She remembered the class making a big deal about the eating habits because Mrs. Huffity said that dragons liked to eat their prey live, the same as spiders. Ivy couldn't help but think it was a poor comparison now that she got a look at a dragon. The dragon really was cute.

"Can I call Carrie?"

Her mom raised her eyebrows, "Are you sure it's not too early?"

"She'll be up for school, too, at least at first. I really need to talk to her."

Ivy took the phone and backpack up to her room and shut the door. It took a few rings until a bleary voice answered, "Hello?"

"It hatched." Ivy unzipped her bag and peeked in at the little dragon who now lay curled into a tight ball at the bottom.

"Ha.Ha. Thanks for waking me up." Carrie still sounded half asleep.

"Carrie, I need your help. I left the instructions in class, and she hasn't eaten yet. I remember Mrs. Huffity saying something about dragons preferring live prey, but I didn't pay attention." Ivy pulled herself onto the bed and stared at the ceiling, one hand on the backpack and one with the phone to her ear.

"Are you seriously serious?" Carrie asked.

"Deadly serious." Ivy said.

"Okay, I'm coming over. If you don't have anything like insects to feed her, she'll eat raw meat. Mrs. Huffity said hamburger would work, although it wasn't exactly healthy for her. But since we're desperate."

"And insects are healthy?" Ivy shook her head. She couldn't believe she was having this conversation.

"According to Mrs. Huffity, anyway. I'm coming over. I'll bring some meat in Ziploc bag. We had hamburger for dinner and my mom has some raw left in the refrigerator."

"Good. I'm a little nervous having her here and I don't know what I'm doing."

They hung up and Ivy waited. Carrie would probably be walking and their families lived three blocks from each other so it would take about twenty minutes for Carrie to get there, counting time to get ready. Ivy yawned and checked on the dragon and waited.

Chapter 7

Ivy's phone call was the best possible thing that could happen to Carrie on the worst morning she'd ever had. Yesterday evening she had answered the door to Tom, one of her parent's friends. He had a large envelope and asked if her mother was home. Carrie yelled up the stairs for Mom and in two minutes whatever happiness and contentment she and her mom had found in each other's company was gone.

Her dad had filed divorce papers. Her mom was especially angry that Tom was the one to serve her, which meant he actually brought the divorce papers to her for Dad. Her mom yelled at Tom. She told him to get out of her house and never come back.

Even though Carrie knew her parents sometimes argued to the point where they couldn't even stand to be in the same room together, she thought they would find a way to make up. Isn't that what people did? They fought and became friends again. Not this time. Not her parents.

Her mom was asleep. Carrie had awoken at three and

heard noise in the kitchen. She went downstairs to find her mom in the middle of a cupboard cleaning project with cans on the kitchen table and spread across the counters and her mom scrubbing the wood inside the cupboards. Now, four hours later, her mom's door was closed and the house was quiet.

Pulling out a piece of notebook paper, Carrie wrote a quick note. *No school for snow. Went to Ivy's at 7:30. Please call when you wake up. I love you. Carrie.*

Grabbing her coat, and pulling her hat on over her head, Carrie hurried out the door. *A dragon hatching. I wonder what Ivy is talking about.*

Carrie ran most of the way. The snow was thick and crunchy and her boots made a thwacking sound as she ran. By the time she got to Ivy's house, she was out of breath. She walked past the last few houses.

She took off her boots in the foyer and ran up the stairs in her socks, waving at Ivy's mom, Trina, on the way.

Ivy heard her coming and opened her bedroom door. "Come check this out."

Her bean bag chair was shoved up against the wall. Carrie's mouth dropped open. There really *was* a dragon hatchling, lifting her head up from the chair to stare at

Carrie. Carrie said, "That's so cool."

The hatchling cried out a rather pathetic mewling sound. Ivy knelt by the chair and pet the dragon's head. "Don't cry. I'm here. I think she's hungry. Did you remember the burger?"

Carrie pulled out a hamburger patty stuffed into a sandwich bag. She handed it to Ivy. "Hope she likes it."

Ivy took a pinch of burger and held it over the dragon's head. She was a little worried that the dragon would snap and hurt her fingers, but the dragon stretched out her neck and held open her mouth, nuzzling her hand while Ivy dropped the burger. "Do you want to try?"

Carrie stared at the dragon and then at Ivy. She couldn't even believe this was real. "I'd like to."

The girls took turns feeding the dragon until the hamburger was half gone. When she didn't want more, the little dragon turned her head and rolled up into a ball.

Ivy shrugged, "Guess she's done."

The girls took turns washing up in the bathroom and Ivy snuck the burger down to the refrigerator, coming back with two orange juices. Carrie always got to drink sodas at her own house. They sat watching the dragon sleep.

"What's her name?" Carrie asked.

"I don't know. I haven't thought of one yet."

Stretching out on the floor with her chin on her hands, Carrie watched the sleeping creature. "Suppose she already has a name?"

"Who would name her?"

"The mama dragon?" Carrie wondered if the egg had been abandoned. It might be a little scary to see a full-sized dragon.

"Maybe we can name her, too." Ivy put out a finger and scratched the place above the dragon's ear where dogs liked to be scratched. The dragon yawned and opened her eyes once before sighing and putting her head back down.

"Maribel Gingledaisy?" Carrie giggled.

Ivy smirked, "Hortensia Minnie Scale"

"Gertrude Firebreath"

"Smokey Nostrellia"

"Ewwww..." Carrie laughed.

Ivy smiled down at the little dragon. "I wish I could think of something stately and proper, something that a dragon could grow into."

The dragon yawned, a long row of teeth widening as the little creature sighed. With a little hiccough, a spark shot from the dragon's mouth.

Carrie's mouth dropped open and she stared. "She breathes fire, just like the stories say."

"We'll call her Sparky. Just for now until we can think of something better." Ivy nodded firmly, her mind set. The girls spent the morning petting her scales, which felt strangely soft and smooth. Later Carrie pulled out the rest of the hamburger and the dragon finished it.

After a few hours Carrie's mom called for her. The girls ran down the stairs giggling as Carrie reached for the phone.

"Mom, can Carrie stay the night?" Ivy put on her best toothy smile, the one her mom just couldn't resist.

"You've got school tomorrow, so you'll have to go to bed early." Her mom narrowed her eyes and looked from one girl to the other. Ivy had the feeling that she knew something was afoot. What her mom didn't know was that the foot was attached to wings, a snout, and large lovely eyes.

Ivy grinned. "We will."

"Okay then."

Ivy tugged on Carrie's sleeve. "Ask if you can stay the night."

Carrie asked, but from the "But Mom." and the disappointed frown, Ivy knew the answer was no.

After hanging up Carrie grumbled, "She was really mad that I left the house this morning. I'm to go straight home before she goes to work. She'll probably yell at me since Dad's not home to yell at."

"I'm sorry." Ivy gave her friend a hug, and even though it pained her to ask, she thought it only fair to share. After they were out of earshot Ivy whispered, "Do you want to take Sparky home with you tonight?"

Carrie brightened. "Really, you'd let me take her?"

"Sure. I've got an old coat you can wrap her in so she'll be warm. You can hide her in the purple backpack until you're home."

"Mrs. Huffity will probably take her back tomorrow. Are you really really really sure?"

Ivy pushed her glasses back up the bridge of her nose and shrugged, "My mom is home all day today, so I'll have more trouble feeding her, anyway."

With Ivy's backpack across her shoulder, Carrie pulled on her gloves. The dragon was heavy. She felt like she was carrying a giant stone in her pack. At least Sparky was quiet.

The girls laughed and looked around for adults when a gurgling sound came from the pack. Once Carrie was gone, the house felt really quiet. Ivy went upstairs to remove any evidence of the little dragon, but she discovered that all of the egg shells were gone, eaten by the gollivants and only the normal messes were left.

The idea that every trace of the dragon could be gone so quickly left Ivy feeling a tinge of sadness.

Chapter 8

Carrie spent the day with the dragon curled up on her lap. She lay on the couch with a nest of pillows and blankets. The two watched television together once her mother had gone to work. Oddly, the little dragon seemed to know things. When Carrie was flipping through channels and an old *Land Before Time* movie was on, Sparky lifted her head and trilled.

"But it's an old movie." Carrie said, "As old as my parents."

Sparky's disappointed mewling made Carrie feel just the slightest bit sorry for the dragon. Finally, she said, "Fine, we'll watch cartoons."

She flipped the channel back to the dinosaur movie.

Petting the dragon's head eased Carrie's worries with her mom and dad and everything that had been happening lately.

"I'm so glad you're here." Carrie said.

She was surprised when the dragon licked her cheek with a sandpapery tongue and said, "Me too."

The dragon's words had not been spoken aloud, but she somehow heard them just the same.

"You're too little to talk." Carrie itched the top of the dragon's head with her fingernail.

"I can't teleport or breathe fire yet, but I can talk to your hearing nerves. Talk is easy because I remember myself before the egg."

That got Carrie's attention and she paused the television. "What are you talking about?"

The dragon tilted her head. "About hearing nerves?"

"No, before you were an egg." Carrie lifted her head a little to look down fondly at Sparky.

"Once I was the size of this planet and I flew through the universe to the most bitter places where even the ice is cold. Dragons warm themselves from the inside. It's very handy for cold."

"How did you come to be tiny and inside an egg?" Carrie was petting the dragon's head the way she would a puppy. It felt soothing to have someone to care for.

"I don't rightly remember, although it had something to do with a star exploding. I suppose I wasn't being terribly cautious at the time."

"But if a star exploded..." Carried cringed at the idea

of the little dragon in the path of a fireball.

"Exactly..." The dragon nodded.

"Exactly what?"

"What you saw in your mind. Your imagination comes close."

"Oh, sorry." Carrie said, even if it wasn't her fault. "Do you want to talk about something else?"

"Would you have more of those tasty little frozen cubes?" The dragon's tongue shot out and licked from one end of her snout to the other.

Carrie had opened a package of frozen stew meat earlier. Sparky ate the whole thing, "No, I think we might need to go shopping."

"It's okay. I can wait a while."

The phone rang, and Carrie looked at the number. Her Dad! "Hi Daddy."

"Hey Princess, I'm sorry I wasn't able to see you this weekend."

"It's okay." Part of her thought it really wasn't. Her mom was making things really hard. Every time Dad called, she'd make nasty comments about him while Carrie was on the phone, and when Mom answered herself, she'd start crying or yelling at him. Carrie hadn't seen his new place now that he was living across town. She asked hopefully, "Will I stay with you this Saturday?"

"I'm sorry, Baby. I'm so busy with getting settled in. The next few weekends aren't great for me, but we'll spend some extra time at Christmas, okay?"

Carrie's eyes filled with tears, but she made her voice sound happy when she said, "That sounds great."

"Take care of yourself."

"I will. You too." With the connection gone, Carrie let the tears fall freely. Sparky rested her head on Carrie's knee and Carrie pet her scales, soft and warm, not at all what she would expect while she cried.

"He loves you." Sparky's words made Carrie feel a little better.

"He's never said it to me." Carrie sniffled and wiped a tear away from her cheek.

"He did. It's just been too long for you to remember. He's afraid you'll hate him, the way your mother does. It makes the words harder." Sparky closed her eyes as Carrie scratched the scales behind her ear.

"Mom doesn't hate him. She's just upset, but she loves him. She has to."

Sparky lifted her head and looked Carrie in the eye

and in those ancient eyes, Carrie couldn't help but see thousands of years of wisdom. "Love is a fragile thing, Carrie. It can die in a cold heart. Your mother has only anger left for your father."

Carrie felt a new flood of tears. She desperately wanted her parents back together. She'd been thinking through all sorts of schemes that might work. She'd even arranged a dinner between the two, only to have her mother cancel at the last minute when she found out what Carrie was doing.

Sparky was telling the truth. Carrie knew it, but she didn't really want to hear it right now. Sparky seemed to know that Carrie needed time to think and quietly lent her support by resting her head on Carrie's knee.

The phone rang at six. It was her mom who wouldn't be coming home right after work.

"I shouldn't be surprised." Carrie said. She felt a longing for sleep, just to turn off her mind and not think about her troubles for a while. But Sparky was there and she didn't want the little dragon to get bored.

"It's okay. I'm tired, too. We can sleep early."

They fell asleep little imagining the trouble they would find upon awakening.

Chapter 9

Carrie awoke to Sparky's muffled cries and strong hands pulling her out of bed in the middle of the night. She couldn't see who was dragging her out or what was going on. It took a moment after awakening to realize what was happening.

She started yelling, "Mom! Help! Mom!"

"Carrie, are you okay?" She heard Sparky's voice in her mind.

"I'm fine." Carrie twisted and turned, "I just can't get away."

Something happened. There was no flash, no sound, nothing to warn her of the change. Just the smell of a damp forest where her bedroom used to be. One moment she was struggling in her bedroom where a night light lit the edge of her bookshelves, the next she was in a mist wondering what had happened.

The hands let go, and Carrie dropped to the ground. She stood and turned to see who had grabbed her, but there was no one there. And worst of all, there was no Sparky either. "Mom?" Carrie didn't say it too loud. It was more of a tentative question that she sent into the mist where it echoed. "Sparky?"

She turned in a circle. The entire world seemed to be made of fog and she was standing on a mossy patch under a cedar tree. The hill sloped, but she couldn't tell how steep in was.

Carrie shivered. She was barefoot and wearing her pajamas. It would have been nice if they had given her a coat, but whoever grabbed her couldn't be bothered with niceties. She started to wonder if they'd dropped her on accident, and then she wondered if they'd be back.

She ran. Her bare feet hurt with every step, but Carrie was frightened enough to ignore the pain and keep on running.

It wasn't until she'd already changed directions twice that it occurred to her that maybe there was a portal that brought her to this world, and maybe she could only get back and forth from the very place where she entered. But it was too late.

Carrie walked and walked, her sleeves catching on branches, her feet cut by small rocks and bits of wood.

Walking down the slope, Carrie heard the sound of a river or waterfall somewhere in the distance. She moved diagonally to the sound of the water. "Ow, ow, ow, ow" With every step, her tender feet landed on something uncomfortable. At least the ground was warmer than home.

A shadow raced by, almost like a flicker in the corner of her eye. Carrie turned, trying to see. She was knocked over, tackled by something furry and large. Her face was in a pile of leaves and twigs, and she could taste the ground. "Bleh." Spitting out dirt, Carrie pulled herself up and tried to find her attacker, but the forest was quiet.

"Hello?" Her voice shook, barely above a whisper. Angry at herself for sounding so frightened, Carrie brushed off her pajama bottoms, her favorite pink princess pajama bottoms, which were now covered in mud.

A face peered out from behind a tree and growled, showing long canine teeth. Carrie stepped back cautiously. One foot at a time, she moved slowly away, trying to put distance between herself and the snarling beast. It was nothing like any animal she'd ever seen with a snout like a pig, but human eyes, intelligent eyes, and long furry arms that ended with furry fingers.

The creature moved forward as Carrie moved back,

stalking her. She turned to run. Before she could take two steps, something had pushed her down. The animal stood on top of her snapping his teeth at her ear and snarling. Three more of the beasts came from out of the trees where they'd been hiding. Two carried weapons. "Don't move."

She could barely understand the words. They came out as a growl, but they were real words. "Who are you?"

Carrie waited for some kind of answer, but she found her arms being held back and strong cords wrapping around her wrists. When she pulled away, one of the creatures snarled and pushed her down. She banged her knee on a stump. A hand wrapped around her throat and she felt herself choking. Until that moment she'd been more angry than afraid. As she lost consciousness, she wondered if her dad would miss her.

* * *

The cage was made of smooth wood and she couldn't stand completely straight inside. A parade of beasts wandered by, a few young ones pointed and grunting as if she were in some kind of zoo. Carrie's head hurt and her knee ached. Her hands were untied so she rubbed the aching part. The bruise was big enough to feel lumpy.

A platter of grass and bowl of water waited in the corner of the cage, and Carrie realized that it was meant to be her food. Her throat felt parched. Stiffly, she half-stood with her head brushing the smooth wooden roof. She limped to the bowls. Cries and squeals arose from the beasts outside and a few furry fingers were pointed in her direction as she knelt by the water.

She lifted the bowl and smelled the water. It didn't smell like swamps or creek water. It actually smelled really good, like clean filtered water. Still, she wasn't thirsty enough yet to drink when she didn't know where it came from. They probably filled it up straight out of a river, and who knows what creatures lived in the water.

Her lips felt so dry. She carefully set the bowl back on the floor. She went to the edge of the cage, watching the room for anyone who might understand her or in some way be helpful. There was no one who would help.

She curled up on the floor. With the dozens of beasts outside the cage, even if she tried to find a way out now, they would just find a new cage for her. She decided to be quiet and think, pretending to be asleep. Closing her eyes, Carrie took inventory. She had no tools, no shoes. The cage was wooden and might be breakable if she had something strong, which she didn't.

Sparky had disappeared. The dragon may or may not know where she was. Whatever happened to Sparky, she had felt the little dragon's dismay when everything happened. It wasn't fear exactly, but then it seemed that dragons probably didn't feel fear that much. Something grabbed Sparky, too. So she couldn't count on rescue.

Carrie opened her eyes and stared at the ceiling of her cage. She didn't want to be one of those kids in the newspapers. Everyone would think she ran away because her parents were getting divorced. They wouldn't know she was trapped in a strange place with strange hairy people holding her captive.

She had to find a way to escape. The cage should have some kind of door. When she was at the zoo, the elephant keeper said that their elephants didn't like humans. They had to use a series of gates so that the elephants could be cared for without ever having human contact. Otherwise, the elephants might hurt their caretakers. Carrie thought about her actions. If she didn't plan carefully, they might put her in a cage like the elephants, a place where she would never find escape.

The crowds dwindled and the lights were dimmed. Eventually Carrie found herself alone in the room. She started in the corner of the cage. Grasping the wooden bar at the corner, she twisted and pushed. The cage was solid. She walked slowly around the edge, testing each bar. When she reached the door, she pushed it forward, her attention on the outer latch. It was a simple hook, the kind her neighbor used in his dog kennel.

She pushed her hand through the bar, her fingers just brushing the edge of the latch. The hook was just out of reach. Carrie decided to keep exploring the cage and come back to the latch. She finished her walk, testing everything until she arrived back at the first corner. The food dish caught her eye. Picking up the saucer, Carrie dumped the grass on the floor, then maneuvered it between the bars.

She hooked the latch on the edge and lifted. Halfway up it slipped. This happened again and again until she was gritting her teeth in frustration. With a quick shove she hefted the saucer up, catching the hook and thrusting it out of the latch until it fell with a clang.

Carrie moved away from the door, scanning the entryways for signs that someone had heard the sound. When no one appeared, she pushed the door open. At least their cages had all the sophistication of a dog house. Anything more secure and she might not have escaped.

I'm not out of here yet. Carrie reminded herself. She had never been good at tiptoeing, but she gave it her best, moving slowly and quietly into the hall and carefully waiting as she passed openings in the hallway.

She heard footsteps coming from around the corner. Seeing an empty alcove, she slipped inside. She hurried as quietly as she could down the narrow hall and quickly ran up the winding staircase. The steps were made of stone and wound in a great circle. Carrie couldn't see beyond the first few steps and decided to keep going. Her logical voice kept telling her to go back. No way would a staircase going up lead to an escape. She'd be better off turning around. But the more she climbed, the more she wanted to see the top.

The stair ended at a large oak door with iron locks and a chain wrapped around the handle. A key hung on a hook next to the door. Carrie took the key and pushed it into the lock. She tried to turn it, but the key stuck. Jamming it in, Carrie jiggled the key back and forth. She growled at it the way her dad did when he was working under the hood of his car trying to unfasten a difficult bolt.

The lock seemed to screech when it gave way and

Carrie froze, listening for the shouts or footsteps running up the stairs to get her. No one heard. With a sigh of relief, Carrie pulled the iron catch down and removed the lock and then the chains.

Opening the door was as difficult as unlocking it. The door was much too heavy for Carrie. She had to put all of her weight into pushing it to make it open. One more grunt with a lot of energy and the door gave way with a lurch. She stumbled into an elegant room.

"Oh!" A girl about the age of Carrie's baby sitter was at a vanity mirror picking through jewelry. Carrie's stomach did a flip-flop when she realized the woman's skin was so translucent that she could see her bones and the eye sockets behind her eyes. The whole effect made her feel queasy.

"Um...sorry about that." Carrie said uneasily, "I guess I'll just be going now."

"But you rescued me. Surely you won't leave me here alone?"

"Rescued? But the room is so pretty." And it was. A deep blue carpet, thick and lush, gave the room a peaceful feeling. A four post bed with blue and gold curtains sat in one corner of the room while the elegant mirror sat in another.

"So you're just another bored maiden out for a jaunt, hoping that the prisoner will entertain you. Well, I'll just have you know that I won't do it. No dancing. No singing. And no stories." She threw her brush onto the table and scowled. Her cheeks were an angry pink strangely overshadowed by the skeletal features beneath the skin.

Carrie looked over her shoulder, hoping the girl's voice didn't carry. "Shh...I'm a prisoner, too. I just escaped and I'm looking for a way out of the castle."

"Well, I'd say you went the wrong way."

For a moment, Carrie felt very much like storming out of the room, locking the door again and leaving the girl to her fate. After all, she *had* been snotty, and Carrie was only trying to help. But Carrie couldn't imagine being locked up all the time, even in a pretty room with no friends to visit and no toys to play with.

"I just wanted to see where the stairs led. I'm going to escape now. Would you like to join me?"

Lifting herself from the chair and picking up her frilly skirts so they wouldn't drag across the ground, the young woman said, "Fine."

"What's your name?" Carrie asked.

"One doesn't address a princess unless first spoken to.

And my name is Minerva." Daintily tiptoeing to the door, Minerva looked back, "Well, aren't you coming?"

Carrie wanted to laugh when Minerva fell back after a short tug at the door. But she didn't. Instead she said, "It's a heavy door. Maybe if we both pull on it."

The princess sniffed, "Of course."

Carrie followed her out the door and down the stairs, not saying a word. Not because the princess had some stupid rule about speaking, but because she didn't want to be caught. Minerva seemed to know quite well where she was going. At the bottom of the tower, she pushed on a stone that looked like a perfect part of the wall. A passageway opened on the wall, this time with stairs leading down.

Carrie looked into the dark stairwell. "What's this?"

"The way out. Are you coming?" Minerva's voice was silky smooth and she seemed to glide across the floor, so upright and stiffly did she walk. Carrie felt like a stork beside her.

"Right behind you."

Carrie wondered how she'd landed in such a big mess. Ivy would never believe what happened to her. Not in a million years! But then, who would have thought that a dragon egg could hatch?

Chapter 10

Ivy couldn't sleep. She wanted to know how Sparky was doing. Was she eating? Did she miss Ivy? What if she thought of Ivy as her mother and got scared...or lonely? Ivy turned back to her other side with a sigh and flipped her pillow. Lifting her head, she looked at her clock and the steady red lights reading ten o'clock. An hour past bed time. Carrie would be asleep. Or awake with Sparky, but either way she couldn't call.

It was another hour before Ivy fell asleep. When she did her dreams were worse than ever. She dreamed that Carrie was in a dark world full of skeletons with glowing eyes. Her dream shifted to Sparky, who was in more danger. The little dragon was on a cliff thousands of feet in the air with her wings torn and bleeding and pinned to cracks in the rock by what looked like climber's gear. Sparky was much larger now, so Ivy thought maybe she was mixing up time with her visions.

When she awoke, only a few hours had passed. She

pushed down the covers to look at the clock, which read midnight. The night was so quiet. Snow tended to muffle sound and keep people indoors, making the world a peaceful place to be. After an hour of tossing and turning, Ivy decided to get dressed and sneak over to Carrie's house.

Getting past her father was the hard part. Her mom was a heavy sleeper and could sleep through a storm, but if she went downstairs for a glass of milk, her father would often be waiting at the top of the stairs when she returned, just to make sure all was well. Her coat and boots were in the downstairs closet. She would have to get down the hall, to the closet, pull on her boots, and open the front door, all without making a sound. Ivy grumbled to herself, "If this were summer, I'd have a better chance."

Her favorite pair of jeans was dirty and in the hamper. Ivy pulled them out and the shirt she had worn two days before. She figured if she got out new clothes, her mom was bound to ask about them. Parents could be really nosey sometimes. She put on the thick wool socks that she liked to wear when she went sledding and grabbed her watch.

"Well, here goes." Ivy whispered into the night.

The heavy socks made tiptoeing down the hallway carpet easier than Ivy expected. She had no idea how heavy she normally walked. She put one foot carefully in front of the other. That tiny walk to the stairs seemed to take forever. She paused between steps, waited and waited, then took another step. Pause. Step. Pause Step.

And then she reached the stairs. Again, she took one step at a time. After another eternity, she reached the bottom of the stairs. The buzzing of the refrigerator seemed oddly comforting after the stress of her latest dreams, and she found herself wondering if maybe the dream was just a regular, ordinary dream. Maybe she should just go back to bed.

But then she remembered seeing the egg in David's locker both in her dream and then in real life. Her dreams sometimes meant something. Creeping along the hall at a snail's pace, Ivy finally reached the closet door, grateful for the night light that illuminated the door knob clearly. She turned it in a swift careful motion and pulled the door open slowly.

Even with the light, her boots were in the recesses of the closet in shadow. Ivy pulled on her coat, deciding to zip it outside and grabbed her boots. Sitting across from the nightlight, Ivy tugged on her boots, careful not to grunt. The last few steps were the worst. Boots were not exactly created for sneaking about.

The best feeling was opening the door and stepping out into the bitter cold. She made it! Somehow she had managed to get all the way downstairs, put on her boots, and walk outside without her father hearing. They lived in a small town and never locked the house up which made getting out the front door in silence much easier. Shutting the door quietly behind her, Ivy hurried across the yard, her boots crunching softly in the snow.

Ivy might have turned back if she'd known that her dad heard the door's click and with a frown and a yawn, dragged himself out of bed to see what was going on. He discovered that she had left the house just as she was turning the corner of Payton Street, two blocks down.

The lights were off at Carrie's house and Ivy came to the conclusion that she had overreacted. All was well.

A hand on her shoulder startled her and Ivy screamed.

"Sorry, honey. Didn't know I was sneaking up on you." Mrs. Huffity removed her hand from Ivy's shoulder with a look of apology behind those large glasses and examined her nails for a moment the way the secretaries in the old movies do after filing them.

"You did, but it's okay. Why are you here?" Ivy

couldn't believe her teacher was standing right here in front of her. It was the strangest thing ever. But then Mrs. Huffity was pretty weird herself, although Ivy liked her anyway.

"You know some things." Mrs. Huffity used that deep and distant voice again.

"I had a dream. Well, two really." Ivy told Mrs. Huffity about Carrie and Sparky, about the skeletons and cliff in her dream and how she snuck out of the house. She finished with, "But Carrie's house is quiet, and I'm sure I made a mistake."

Mrs. Huffity pushed her glasses back and squinted into the night and for a moment Ivy would swear she was sniffing the air. "Not a mistake at all. No. Carrie is not in the house. Neither is Sparky."

"What about Carrie's mom?" Ivy couldn't believe Carrie's mom would be asleep if Carrie was gone.

"Asleep. At least for now. I don't doubt she'll notice until Carrie is gone in the morning." Mrs. Huffity swiveled around slowly, scanning the streets. It gave Ivy a rather creepy feeling, as if Mrs. Huffity were stalking prey or something. It seemed like a very animal-like way to move.

"Um...Mrs. Huffity?" Ivy asked.

"Yes?" Mrs. Huffity murmured.

"What are you doing?"

Mrs. Huffity turned once more, this time scanning the sky. "We're going to find Carrie and Sparky. Now, don't be frightened." Mrs. Huffity said quietly. "It's my fault the girls are in danger."

And then Mrs. Huffity was gone. From standing not three feet from Ivy to complete and utter nothingness. Ivy couldn't believe it. She turned in a circle of her own, blinking her eyes and shaking her head to see if she could wake herself up. A taloned claw grasped her shoulder and Ivy found herself in a warm meadow filled with flowers and stars that she'd never seen before. Half of the sky was blotted out. Ivy wondered how it changed so fast from winter to spring and why the sky was filled with unfamiliar stars, Ivy said, "Are we in Australia?"

She heard a rumbling laughter and realized it was coming from a rather large shadow blocking out the stars, far above her head.

"Mrs. Huffity?" Ivy called, hoping her teacher hadn't gone too far.

"Up here." The deep voice said.

A large face bent down from the great heights at the top of the shadow. Ivy realized the shadow was really a dragon, a huge dragon with large purple wings and sharp talons. Ivy stared. "Are you really a dragon?"

"Yes. I'm sorry for the deception. Now, if you're ready, I'd like you to climb up. I need your help freeing Sparky." Mrs. Huffity in dragon form seemed very large, almost scary, but the way she talked about Sparky, Ivy knew Mrs. Huffity loved the little dragon. And since Ivy was fond of Sparky herself, she decided not to let fear make the decision.

"How do I get up there?" Ivy asked, feeling curiously unafraid. Her teacher was a dragon. Ivy supposed that a bit of screaming or hiding under the bed was called for, but she couldn't help but remember Mrs. Huffity tapping her forehead or the warnings to Carrie. The dragon was on her side.

Still, Ivy felt a small measure of embarrassment climbing the scaly leg. The scales were thick and bumpy enough that she could use them as hand and foot holds. The only time Ivy felt afraid was when the dragon stretched her neck and turned to look at her. The deep voice rumbled, "We must hurry."

Ivy nearly lost her grip with that giant blue-green eye staring at her. Mrs. Huffity's eyes were not that color of sea-green. Ivy was sure of that. A small saddle sat on the dragon's neck, complete with harness. It gave Ivy some feeling of comfort. The saddle had a tall back, stirrups and a saddle horn just like cowboys used when they did cow-roping in the rodeos.

"Get strapped in. We're ready for lift-off."

The seat also had an attached harness that amusement parks used for roller coasters, the kind that went up over the head. The buckle ended at the front the way a baby carrier does. It took a minute for Ivy to figure out how to get the contraption on properly. When she was finally buckled in, the dragon leapt into the air and Ivy felt her stomach do a flip-flop. She whooped and laughed, leaning over the dragon's shoulder to watch the tree-tops pass by in a blur.

"This is one of my favorite worlds." Mrs. Huffity said.

Ivy was glad she wore a coat. Even with the blue-white sun and the white sky, the air rushing into her face was chilly.

"I thought the blue and white stars were the hottest?" Ivy said, thinking of the lesson they had just covered two weeks ago. Mrs. Huffity didn't like to teach out of the book and went to great and imaginative lengths to describe every kind of star. Now Ivy thought that perhaps those vivid descriptions came from personal experience.

"Yes, they are." Mrs. Huffity said. "But not to worry, this star is actually further out. You wouldn't believe how long a year is on this planet, but the rotations work out to make a nice comfortable place to fly."

They flew over a desert, then over water and Ivy decided she would never be excited to take a plane again. As they flew, Mrs. Huffity pointed out mermaids, although when she looked, Ivy thought they looked just like fish or dolphins from a distance. Every now and then she could see the flash of a fin or the flip of a tale, but not once did she really get a good look at their faces.

And then they were back over land and tall mountains, flying along the coast above mountains and water. "We're almost there." The dragon said.

Ivy didn't really get a good look at the cliff in her dream. Now that she was really here, she could see the sheer wall of rock, a cliff face hanging out over the ocean where fierce waves pounded the shore.

Sparky thrashed at two very sharp, thick bolts pierced right through the membranes of her wings. The little dragon bawled, her trumpeting cries piercing the air while she struggled against the bolts, trying to pull her wings away and tearing more of the membrane while she did.

Mrs. Huffity murmured a strange language. The words sounded musical, but Ivy couldn't understand what was said. But Sparky calmed down and her expression changed from one of terror to waiting.

"I'm going to fly as close to Sparky as I can. There are tools in the pocket of the seat. "You'll need to pull out the stakes." The dragon's voice sounded angry as they hovered. Ivy didn't blame her. She felt angry herself.

Mrs. Huffity roared.

Ivy shivered, partly from the cold sea air blowing up the cliff face and partly from the dragon's temper. She decided right then that she would never talk out of turn in class, always volunteer when Mrs. Huffity asked, and NEVER send Carrie notes EVER again.

Ivy? She heard Mrs. Huffity's voice in her head.

"I'm ready. What do I do now?" Ivy asked, while tears slid down her cheeks. The little dragon was so close that Ivy could touch her, and Ivy could see the dragon skin stuck to the pikes and the drops of green blood dripping down the wing and falling ever so far into the great sea below.

"Don't unhook yourself yet. Reach down into the pocket. There is a rope there. I want you to tie it around yourself and then onto the saddle horn you've been gripping." Mrs. Huffity held steady, the way a helicopter hangs in the air on television shows.

Ivy pulled the rope out of the bag. A loop was already knotted into one end in a slip-knot. She put the rope over the saddle horn and pulled it taut, then wrapped it around her waist, struggling with numb fingers to get it tied.

"Be careful with that knot. Make sure it's tight."

Ivy could hear Mrs. Huffity's teacher voice somewhere in the depth of the dragon and nodded solemnly. "I will."

"Your life may depend on it." The dragon turned her head and trilled to Sparky who had stopped struggling and whose body sagged on the stakes while she waited. Sparky trilled back.

"Rope is tied. Shall I unbuckle my harness?" Ivy asked.

"Not yet. Try to pull out the stakes while sitting. A dragon doesn't have the kind of strength in that part of the wing to use much force against the spike."

Ivy leaned over the saddle and reached for the first one. "I'm sorry, Sparky."

In her mind she heard a comforting thanks and assurance and felt some comfort knowing that Sparky trusted her. Ivy grasped the spike with both hands and pulled, but sitting as she was couldn't get the leverage she needed. "I think I have to unhook myself."

Be careful. She heard Sparky's warning in her mind.

"I will." Ivy unbuckled the harness and closed her eyes, taking a deep breath to calm herself. She lifted a leg over the saddle horn and wedged it against one of Mrs. Huffity's dark scales, "Here goes."

Grasping the stake with both hands, Ivy pulled with all her might. The spike pulled free from the crack in the rock and then out of Sparky. Sparky squawked and fluttered, falling a few inches which further tore the wing still caught on the cliff. Mrs. Huffity's tail stopped Sparky from doing more damage. Sparky's wing bled freely and Mrs. Huffity tilted her tail so that Sparky would feel less strain on the wing still trapped.

"The darkness is coming," Sparky said. She was looking out into the distance. Mrs. Huffity's head whipped around so fast that Ivy nearly lost her balance and had to grab the saddle horn.

"Ivy, you need to hurry. Get that other wing clear." Mrs. Huffity spoke quietly and with that quiet certainty that reminded Ivy of the day her Mom cut her foot really badly, and her father told her to go get a kitchen towel. His voice was just that calm, too. Scary calm.

Freeing Sparky's other wing was more difficult. Ivy had to work around Sparky herself and Mrs. Huffity's tail, all of which was secondary to the sudden change in wind and the distant and fierce cries of the approaching enemy. Ivy's heart beat faster and she stood once more, putting both hands on the spike and pulling. Nothing happened.

"Move it back and forth." Mrs. Huffity said in her deep dragon voice.

You two should get out of here. Sparky spoke in Ivy's mind. Ivy wondered if Mrs. Huffity could hear.

Apparently she could because Mrs. Huffity said, "We're staying. You're almost free. Just hang on."

Ivy pushed the spike up like a lever, cringing when Sparky moaned. She pulled it down and felt the spike loosen. With a sharp tug, Sparky came free.

What happened after that was confusing. Ivy looked up to see Mrs. Huffity wrap her tail around Sparky, holding her safe. Then a dinosaur attacked. It looked like a pterodactyl with razor sharp teeth and long claws. And then Mrs. Huffity moved to avoid a slash, and Ivy slipped.

She felt herself falling and grabbed out, catching a

scale with her right hand. The pterodactyl scored Mrs. Huffity across the back with its long sharp claws and then screamed. That unearthly scream and Mrs. Huffity's swerve shocked Ivy enough that she slipped and found herself dangling over the water, a human piñata.

The knot held, but Ivy's body hurt from being jerked back when her sudden fall was stopped by the rope. She grabbed the rope in her hands and tried to pull herself straight. She watched while three more dinosaurs swooped in an attack pattern on the dragon and then found herself flying closer and closer to the water.

She heard a voice in her head. *Can you swim?*

Yes. Ivy answered back. She and Carrie spent every afternoon during the summer at the pool.

With a sharp twist the dragon flipped in the air, and Ivy found herself falling, a wave of water striking her as she drew a deep breath and held it.

Her coat dragged her down as she fought against the waves. Her jeans made treading water difficult. Before the waterlogged coat could drown her, she unzipped it and pulled her arms out, letting herself sink and hoping that she would have enough air to kick her way up. The tumbling of the water was confusing, but Ivy focused on the one thing in front of her. She had to get out of that coat and then the jeans.

They'd practiced in Advanced Swimming and Life Saving lessons, not that anyone expected Ivy or her friends to save anyone, but they learned to kick off shoes, remove jeans and jacket and make floatation devices out of them. She used that knowledge now and the stray thought that her mom would kill her when she came dragging herself home without coat or shoes gave Ivy that extra certainty that she had to survive. It would be worse if she didn't go home at all. After the shoes and coat were off, Ivy let them fall into the ocean and kicked and swam as hard as she could to the surface, the salt stinging her eyes.

She broke through and took a huge gulp of air before the next wave hit. The blue-white sun seemed to blind her, and while she heard the aerial battle and trumpeting of the dragons and screams of the pterodactyls, she could only focus on keeping afloat and breathing before the next wave hit.

She tread water for a moment trying to get a feel for her surroundings. When she swam along the height of the waves, she saw that the long cliff face across from where she struggled was strewn with large rocks. A mile or so down the way, she spotted a sandy beach where she hoped to make a safe landing.

Are you okay? Ivy sent the thought to Mrs. Huffity.

She heard nothing in response. The jeans she was dragging along resisted her efforts to swim. NO way would she go home without her jeans. They lived in a small town and she'd never live it down.

And if Barry or even worse, if David saw her, well, she would have to move away and change her name. Too bad there wasn't a witness protection program for disasters like this. Ivy thought all of this while swimming, never doubting that she would reach the shore, never doubting that Mrs. H. would win the fight and take her home. She focused on what she could do to save herself and did it.

When she first stood on shaky legs and looked around, she realized that the sounds had stopped, the world had gone silent, and the skies were empty. Ivy was alone, utterly alone, wet and exhausted, without coat or shoes. Ivy walked up the beach and found a spot with a huge warm rock. She hung her jeans on one side of the rock and climbed up to sit on the other side.

"I'm not sure I like this." She said to herself. "No, I'm sure I don't."

She'd always wanted adventure, to travel the world, maybe be an astronaut or work on a submarine, to climb those rickety pathways in Peru and take the trains across Europe. But somehow those adventures seemed safe, maybe because someone had already done them.

She sat in the warm sun searching the skies for Mrs. Huffity or Sparky. The sun warmed her from the chill of the water and lulled her into a sleepy yawn. She found her eyes closing. A rock is no place to sleep and Ivy rubbed her eyes and sat up, yawning again. She stayed in the sun until her hair warmed, and her jeans were dry. Pulling them on, she looked around the strange world and realized how alone she was.

She still ached from the ropes and rubbed her stomach. When she lifted her shirt, large bruises had formed where the harness had caught her. The rope hadn't been that long, but her bruises sure made it seem like a long fall.

Tired from the swim, Ivy decided to find shelter. She walked across the beach, carefully avoiding the rocks while her feet sunk into the sand. Without shoes or a coat, she would need some way to keep warm. Scrubby grass gave way to pine trees, and the sand squishing through her toes turned to dirt and bark.

Walking without shoes was difficult. Ivy realized how sensitive her feet were to every bump, every sharp stone, and every pricker. And she realized for the first time, she was homesick. She'd never wanted home as much as she wanted it right now.

Chapter 11

Following a princess deep into the bowels of the earth
was a hugely bad idea, as Carrie told herself again and again.
They were walking in utter darkness. Minerva had taken
Carrie's hand, and the feel of those strange bony fingers
under hers gave Carrie the creeps. Not to mention stepping
on slime. The girls would be walking on rock one moment
and stepping on slime the next. Carrie imagined slugs and
worms and all kinds of disgusting things under her bare feet,
but she couldn't see a thing. The deeper they went, the more
she wished for the cage she'd just escaped.

"How much further?" Carrie asked.

The princess tightened her grip and Carrie's fingers
felt crunched, "Did I not say that you may speak only when
spoken to?"

"You might have mentioned it, but you're just a kid
like me." Carrie said.

The princess huffed with an exaggerated air of
importance, "From birth I have been raised as royalty. You

are common."

Carrie let go of the princess's hand. "Fine, maybe I'm common, but I still got you out of that room. And I don't care who you are. You go that way. I'll go this way."

"Well!" The princess grumbled as she walked away from Carrie.

Carrie's pride had gotten her into trouble on more than one occasion. Even though she knew she needed the princess's help to see, Carrie didn't care. Alone in the dark, and completely and utterly lost, she kept walking. She wouldn't be treated like she was some loser just because a snotty girl was raised to royalty.

With a hand on the rock, Carrie followed the path back the way they had come. The princess could see quite well without light, having lived all of her life in darkness. Carrie, on the other hand, was blind.

She reached a fork in the pathway. Originally they had come from the left, but Carrie didn't even see the passage or the fork. Without knowing, she went the wrong direction. She was taking each step while she trailed her fingers along the rock, praying for light, praying at each step that she would reach the stairwell. And each step took her deeper into the mountain and further into darkness.

* * *

Minerva stormed down the dark hallways, angry at the
upstart commoner. She stopped before the throne room. It
was hard waiting for the petitioners to finish, but Minerva
knew something of timing. When the last petition had been
heard, the princess glided into the throne room with an air of
superiority that had taken years to perfect, "Father, I have
returned."

The king frowned. This wasn't exactly what he and
King Theo had planned. King Theo was going to set her up
in the tower above the underground and send out word that
he had captured a princess. While he held her captive, King
Glome of the underground had promised marriage to
Minerva's rescuer which would be either Theo's prince if he
thought her pretty or someone King Glome selected. But the
plan failed...and here she was.

"Were you unhappy with King Theo?" he asked.

"Father, I was a prisoner, locked in a tower. And
there was *light* everywhere." Minerva said the word as if it
were the most foul thing she had experienced. To a dark
dweller, it was. Imagine living in a world where the light was

brightened ten-fold.

"Well, you're back and that's what matters. Come show me your husband." King Glome looked around the room while his subjects looked up at the ceiling or down at their feet, anywhere but at him, likely one of them thought they'd be married off to the girl who was rather spoiled.

"How could I get married? I was trapped." The princess put a hand on her hip just above a frilly circlet of lace and lifted her chin. "I would like to have a bath drawn and fresh bedding. Are my royal chambers in order?"

The king looked at his steward who shook his head slightly. "I'm afraid your sister, thinking you were not coming back after so long, moved into your royal chambers. However, we will get you settled into new ones."

Women were forever meddling with kings. It was a fact that very few princes ever came to terms with until they were well entrenched in a marriage, bound forever to the woman who would most meddle with their life. In this case, Minerva's step-mother, Queen Norde, was the culprit who determined empty chambers should not go to waste.

"Ah, I see." The princess curtsied to her royal father, nodded at his steward, and with a lift of her skirts strode gracefully from the room the way women who practiced with books on their heads might. Not that the princess would have learned that way. She was much too proud to wear a book.

"My Lord?" The steward interrupted the king, who was still looking puzzled in the direction of the door which had swung closed.

"I'm sorry, you were saying?"

The steward put a finger to his lips, deep in thought. "The princess never named her rescuer."

"You're right. Ask her right away. We may salvage this yet."

"Do you suppose this means we can send King Theo's daughter back?" The steward asked.

The eyes in King Glome's skeletal sockets glowed brightly for a moment, as if the thought excited him, then sat back and they dimmed. After a long sigh, King Glome, looking very depressed shook his head, "No, a promise is a promise. We don't know how Minerva escaped. Go and see what you can find out about a rescuer."

The steward clicked his heals together in a salute and with a sharp bow left the king's side. The lights in the cavernous hallway were extremely dim, but the man had no trouble navigating the hallways. After all, he was a member of the underworld and could see quite clearly the portraits of King Glome, his father, and his father before him hanging so elegantly in the hallway. The overworlders walked right by the paintings as if they didn't exist.

It took but a moment to find the princess. She had, of course, stopped by the kitchen to pester Cook for treats.

"Princess, I am sorry for bothering you. The king your father would like to reward the man who rescued you." The steward stood at attention while the princess sat at an onyx table eating vanilla custard, a dish imported from the overworld and much favored by the princess.

"It was a girl, not a man. And I don't think you should reward her. She wouldn't bow to me once. She spoke without my permission...and...she's a commoner." The princess whispered in a loud voice, which the commoner cooks and maids couldn't help but overhear as the princess didn't really want to whisper, but only pretend to speak quietly.

"Where is she now?" The steward asked, eyeing another custard dish on a tray on the counter.

"Somewhere roaming the halls. She couldn't see a thing in the dark. I doubt she made it far." The princess scraped the bottom of the custard dish and then licked the spoon.

"And you left her alone?"

"Of course. Why would I follow her into the darkness?

"Thank you, Princess." The steward nodded to the princess once and clicked his heels together. "I must notify the king at once."

The head cook waved with a spoon to the custard dishes, "Must you? I have a custard specially made. You can have it if you'd like."

The steward licked his lips and swallowed, "Surely the girl will be okay another five minutes."

"She will." The princess said.

The steward delicately picked up one of the custards and a spoon and found an out-of-the-way spot by the door to eat. It really did only take five minutes. The steward handed the custard bowl to the kitchen maid washing dishes. "Duty calls. Thank you, my dears."

The cook giggled and the maids curtsied, for the steward was a handsome gentleman, newly appointed to his duties. The steward smiled as he left the kitchen.

The king had left the throne room for the gardens. A variety of lichen and moss grew in a large cavern where water trickled down the walls. He sat on a large rock, watching the water droplets drip...drip...drip.

"Lord King?" The steward waited at the entrance, not wanting to disturb King Glome.

"Come. Tell me the news."

"My plan has failed. Instead of a princely rescue, the princess was saved by another girl, a commoner who apparently does not understand our customs."

"Let's see her." The king tucked his robes into his belt and stepped barefoot into a pool of water.

"The princess left her to wander alone. I've sent several footman to retrieve her."

Sinking into the water with a sigh, the King Glome wriggled his toes. "Perhaps we can marry the rescuer to Troy as a reward."

Troy was the other problem on Glome's mind. A noble with designs on the throne who often hinted in the king's presence that he was lonely and could use a life-long companion.

Chapter 12

At first Carrie wasn't afraid of the dark. As a matter of fact, she felt confident that she would be back at the castle stairs at any moment, but the moments passed and eventually she realized that she had missed a turn somewhere. That's when she started to worry. It wasn't so much the dark itself as that there was no way to remove the darkness, as if she suddenly went blind and didn't know if she'd ever see again.

When a soldier stopped her with a "Halt in the name of the King", Carrie smiled. She couldn't help herself.

"Oh, it is SO good to hear another voice. I've been walking around in the dark forEVER" Carrie couldn't see the soldier in the dark, but his voice was soft and deep and rather comforting after the trying time she'd had.

"The King has been waiting to see you." The soldier walked away, his footsteps quickly fading into the darkness.

"Wait!" Carrie called out. "Where are you going? I can't see a thing out here."

The soldier returned and when she stumbled in the dark, she felt a hand on her arm. The fingers felt strangely hard, more so than a human hand, as if she was feeling bone instead of flesh. "Are you completely blind or just affected by the dark?"

"I can see with light." Carrie said.

The soldier turned on a small lantern. A small flame jumped. It was the cutest little lantern Carrie had ever seen. He held it up for her. In that instant, she caught a glimpse of his face and his eye sockets with burning flames for eyes. She didn't jump or scream. After all, the fellow was being kind to her. Still, it gave her a bit of a shiver. He was more of a skeleton than the princess. Carrie wondered if the princess would look this scary when she grew up.

"Thank you." Carrie was proud of herself for remembering her manners.

Carrie was given refreshments, a lovely custard with a tasty crust and water. After she had been sitting a while, she was summoned to the throne room. King Glome was seated in his royal seat, having just returned from the gardens, and clapped his hands when the guard brought Carrie before him. "What a treat! The woman who saved my daughter. I have the perfect reward."

Carrie didn't know what to do. In all the stories, girls did curtsies and boys bowed, but girls wore dresses and here she was in pajamas. She decided on a curtsy and said, "I don't need a reward, sir."

"Pah," King Glome said, "You shall be married to Lord Troy."

Carrie didn't like where this was going. Betrothed at ten? That was a terrible fairy tale and totally stunk as a reward. "Your Highness, I am too young to be married."

At that moment, the princess entered the royal throne room, her hair piled up. She was dressed in a frilly gown. Carrie had to guess the color since the lantern wouldn't give that much detail. The princess was not happy to see Carrie. "What is she doing here? You fetched her, didn't you? I told you she was rude. I didn't need saving."

Carrie wished that *she* was a princess. Maybe she'd be spoiled and have a father who actually cared about whether she was kidnapped. Carrie snapped at her. "You should be grateful that you have someone who cares about whether you return."

King Glome heard those words with a heavy heart. After all, he had arranged his own daughter's kidnapping and yet this rescuer was giving him credit for caring, which of course he did, but he couldn't manage the princess and certainly didn't know what to do with her. The princess put a hand on her hip and said, "Ooohhhhh, I can't believe you're even talking to her. Daddy, show her to the surface immediately."

The way she said the word *surface*, Carrie knew that the princess thought it a punishment. But she'd love to be shown the surface. She was ready to walk out of this crazy dark world and find the way back on her own.

"Some day, this girl is going to be a royal cousin. I expect you to treat her as such." It was the biggest set down King Glome could give to his royally spoiled daughter and she seemed to draw herself up in anger ready to throw a royal tantrum.

Carrie had no idea what the king would do to her when she spoke her mind. From what she had read, kings often threw people in dungeons for disagreeing with their royal edicts, but a dungeon might be better than what he had in mind for her. "I agree with your daughter. I belong on the surface."

"We'll talk about this after dinner." The king waved his hand to the steward, "Get this girl comfortable chambers, clothes, and food. See that she wants for nothing."

The steward led Carrie through a labyrinth of halls, allowing her the use of that same flickering lantern.

Carrie liked her new room. She jumped on the bed. Her father would have yelled at her, but her father wasn't here. And she was angry. No one listened to her. Not that she should expect a king to listen, but there were limits to what a kid could take. So she jumped, trying to reach the ceiling, which she could barely see anyway in the dim light. At least the steward brought her more candles. The room was awash in candle light and the room was beautiful, stunning even, which surprised Carrie. And she'd taken a bath in hot water.

The dresses were pretty, and this new nightgown she wore felt so soft. She loved touching the fabric. Carrie said, "I can't be bought."

She jumped again and wished that Ivy was here to jump with her. It really wasn't fun breaking the rules alone. The princess opened the door to her room. "There you are. I was told you had bathed and been given a new wardrobe. Are you really going to be my cousin?"

Carrie sprung as high as she could, "No."

The princess shrugged, taking a seat at the vanity. "You should stop doing that. Daddy says you might break through the ceiling and end up in the overworld on the surface if you jump on the bed."

116

Carrie jumped again, "He was lying to you."

The princess straightened her spine and tilted her chin, and with a fierce gaze said, "My royal father does not lie."

The princess had to be at least four years older than Carrie. She wondered how Minerva could be so naïve. "My parents lie all the time. My mom said that we were a happy family and that her arguments with dad didn't mean anything and then he left. He said he'd come see me on the weekends, but half the time he's too busy. I bet your father did lie."

The princess watched Carrie leap again. "How long have you been jumping?"

"Since I got out of the bath. My hair is almost dry." Carrie said, tugging on a strand as she flew into the air.

"And you haven't flown into the overworld?" The princess took a step closer to the bed.

"Not once. Come on, it's really fun." The bed was huge. Carrie bounced back to make room for the princess.

"Do your parents let you jump on the bed?" The princess asked.

"No. I'd get in so much trouble if I did." Carrie said.

"Because you might hop into the overworld?" The princess asked.

"They say I'll break the bed."

"Oh, well, I'll just get another one." Scrambling up, the princess took a test leap. "Hey, this is fun."

The girls pounced and played, tried jumping off the bed onto the carpet, from the carpet onto the bed, and laughed until their sides hurt. When the steward knocked to remind Carrie to change for dinner, the princess helped her change into the pretty blue gown with ribbons and a hoop skirt and helped fix her hair. "I've never had a friend before." The princess said shyly.

"It's because you were taught to be royal." Carrie said, "It's hard to be a friend with someone that you have to bow to."

The princess thought about that. "Is it really?"

Carrie pulled up the strange stockings, which were similar to nylons but thicker. "It really is. Like being friends with a teacher." She thought of Mrs. Huffity. Even the cool teachers were still teachers, and as nice as they might be, they weren't friends.

The princess held out Carrie's shoes. "Don't bow to me ever again. I'd rather play. Please, can we be friends?"

Thinking of Ivy, Carrie realized how lucky she was, how lucky she had always been. This girl lived alone. It didn't matter how much stuff you had or how many servants to fetch things...if you didn't have someone to care about, it was all meaningless. "We'll be great friends."

The girls chatted through dinner, much to the surprise of the royal court and the servants. They had expected the princess to order Carrie about the way she did her cousins.

King Glome whispered to his wife, "What are they talking about?"

"The current conversation is centered around dragons," his wife smiled primly to the ambassador before whispering, "This new friend of hers has dangerous ideas. She seems to think she can befriend a dragon."

Glome laughed, "Don't worry, Dear. It's doubtful she will ever meet one."

The queen didn't share Glome's certainty. She listened to the chatter and wondered where her beloved daughter had gone. Her Minerva had been taught to put people in their proper place. Perhaps the stranger's marriage to a lesser cousin would take care of the problem. Too young? Hah! What commoner could say no to a king?

Chapter 13

The world was deserted. Ivy marched along the edges of the forest where sand met trees and hunted for Carrie or Sparky or Mrs. Huffity. When no one she knew appeared, Ivy looked for anyone else. When Sparky was born, they spoke mind to mind. Ivy decided that if she was ever going to find anyone, that would be the way to do it.

She pressed her eyes together in a squint and thought as hard as she could, "Sparky? Mrs. Huffity?"

Silence. Except for the birds chirping and the insects buzzing.

Ivy was stopped by a rushing river. It was too wide to cross without getting wet again, and the foam where the ocean crashed against the incoming water looked dangerous. A dirt trail followed the river. Ivy turned with the pathway and walked inland.

She trudged along until her legs ached. She kept going even when she got hungry or thirsty. Although the brown river made her mouth water, Ivy could just hear her mother,

Now, Ivy, you kids don't drink the water in the creek no matter how clean it looks. You'll get beaver fever or worse. Ivy didn't quite know what beaver fever was but decided not to take any chances.

Ivy came to a place where two rivers joined to become one large one. She was now climbing away from the river because the water moved too fast and the terrain was so rocky. She had no choice but to take a trail along a cliff above the river.

Someone had carved a bench and set it alongside the trail under a copse of trees near the waterfall. It was an invitation to rest, and Ivy sank down on the seat. The sound of the water splashing on the rocks made her feel quiet inside. Somehow in this quiet expanse, she heard Sparky calling her.

I'm at the waterfall. Ivy told Sparky. *Are you safe?*

We escaped and I'm covered in bandages. I won't be able to move for a couple of days. I can help you find Carrie. She's under the stone.

Ivy was so relieved to hear Sparky's voice that she felt like doing a little dance. *I'll go to Carrie. Tell me what to do.*

It wasn't like getting directions from the internet or a map. As she asked Sparky for directions, Ivy found that sometimes Sparky forgot that she was walking and not flying. A few minutes of fly-time for Sparky could be two hours of walking for Ivy and involve climbing over boulders or along steep and winding paths.

When the sun started to sink, casting orange rays of light through the trees, Ivy panicked. *Sparky, what do I do? I'll be alone here in the dark.*

But she never heard Sparky's advice. Sparky's voice had disappeared.

She continued walking as the sun sank ever so slowly behind the trees. Ivy yawned. Out of the corner of her eye, she saw something dart across her vision and jump into a tree. She tried to snap out of her yawn and look, but by the time her eyes quit watering, there was nothing to see.

"Hello? Anyone there?" Ivy couldn't believe she was going to be spending the night alone in a strange forest with no sleeping bag, no tent, no flashlight, and no book. This was shaping up to be the worst night ever. And that included the night she spent at the hospital when her Mom's appendix burst.

A strange chittering filled the air and a creature burst from behind a tree running at her. At the last minute it changed directions. "Hey, I won't hurt you."

Another creature hopped down from a tree. It looked like a lizard with a giant head and a mouthful of teeth which it immediately used on her arm. Tears in her eyes, Ivy shook off the creature. "Change of plans. I'm going to hurt you."

Grabbing a branch, Ivy hit the lizard over the head. When it backed away, she started stripping the leaves from the bark to make a club. Whatever courage she felt when she survived the dunk in the ocean failed, and she screamed when the next creature came running. It didn't stop.

Ivy swung the branch, pretending the creature was a softball. She was on the softball league last spring. Every Tuesday and Thursday night, they played. She was on the Brownie League. With a hefty swing, she launched the creature into the night. With a gurgle and a scream of its own, the creature flew among the trees, although Ivy was too busy looking for more to see it land.

Her arm was bruised and the skin broken in a few places at the site of the attack. She circled slowly, edging away from the tree limbs above. The forest grew silent as the sky darkened. Ivy called for Sparky as she slowly turned. The darkness would come soon and Ivy realized the creatures weren't leaving. Another one dropped from one of the tree limbs and started running for her. She swung on this one and missed. It ran up to her pant leg and looked ready to launch itself at her face when she kicked it.

Ivy didn't wait to see what else would come. She fled. Running through the forest barefoot, the pads of her feet were cut on rocks and thorns while she tripped and bruised her knees. She ran until she was panting for breath and then ran some more. The creatures stalked her, chasing her through the forest.

She refused to let them herd her like a deer. If a group moved close, she sometimes turned toward them instead of away while she ran. Heaving her stick, she swung at them, sometimes losing her balance and falling. When she did, one or two of the beasts would bite her.

They jumped all over the place, into the trees, out of the trees, over logs. She thought of the piranhas Mrs. Huffity once told her about and wondered if she would survive once they swarmed over her.

When the giant birds started swooping down from the trees, Ivy cried. Bad enough to have those nasty little biters, but with the birds, she had no hope. She kept running, her clothes torn. Everything hurt. And then she realized that the birds weren't swooping at her. They were swooping on the little biting lizards. And the lizards were running.

With a whoop, Ivy thanked the birds. Not that they could understand her. But a little bird soaring among the giants swooped and landed on her shoulder, startling her. *You can come to our nest. If you want to, one of the big birds will give you a ride.*

Ivy wiped tears from her eyes, some of it stress from the little creatures, some of it relief. *Thank you. I would, if you think it's safe.*

The safest. You'll be protected from the little beasts. And you can leave whenever you want. The big ones like flying. They'll be happy to take you wherever you want to go.

Of course a bird would think an aerie a thousand feet in the air was safe. Once Ivy was riding the giant bird, she realized that she was now completely dependent on the birds. She'd never be able to scale down the mountainside on her own. They were miles away from the ocean. When they landed in a huge nest at the top of a craggy section of mountain, Ivy felt very small next to the tall nests. The stars swirled across the sky in a pattern Ivy had never seen before. The sight gave her such a feeling of aloneness. She was lost somewhere in the universe. And the universe was so very big.

Sleep now. The little bird had flown up with Ivy and

was now perched on the side of the nest.

Don't the big ones talk? Ivy asked.

To me, yes. To you, no. You can't see the images fast enough. It would make you feel sick. Sleep now. The bird flew away. The bottom of the nest was soft, filled with downy feathers. Ivy sneezed once, but curled up against the side wall. Her legs hurt where she bruised and scraped them, and with all the excitement she was exhausted.

Ivy would have never guessed that she could fall asleep without a blanket or pillow. But sleep she did. The morning sun and the sound of birds chirping and the guttural caw of the larger birds woke her up.

The sides of the nest were tall, so tall that she had to stand up to see over the edge. Once she did, she was glad the nest felt so sturdy. The space between where Ivy peered over the edge and the ground stretched out in a huge distance. The trees looked like tiny shrubs. Stepping to the middle of the nest, Ivy had to catch her breath. It was so far down. She didn't want to look down any more, but she could hardly help herself. You could see so many things from this height.

It's much safer in the skies. The blue top-knot feather on the little bird bobbed up and down. Ivy was still awe-struck by the distance, but wasn't quite ready to look over the edge again.

How do I get down? Ivy asked. She decided now was as good a time as any to be going.

Well, you can't really. Now that you're here.

But I don't want to stay anymore.

Then jump out. The bird cocked its head and peered at Ivy with one eye.

Ivy crept up to the edge and peered over again. The air seemed colder at this height. *I'll wait until the bigger ones are ready to take me down.*

The little bird laughed. It was a musical sound, a near chirping. Ivy wouldn't have guessed it had any sinister undertones until the bird said, *Why would they take you down? You just got here.*

But you said I'd be safe here and that I could leave whenever I wanted. Ivy was getting tired of having a conversation in her head with the bird. It was making fun of her with images of her falling and splatting on rocks or of a thousand little creatures biting her.

I lied. The bird fluttered it's wings and hopped once. *So get yourself settled in. You'll be making a home of this place for a while.*

Ivy couldn't believe what she was hearing. *And then what? You can't keep me here forever.*

Not forever. Just until the eggs hatch. The little bird turned its head toward another nest a short distance away.

Ivy was thinking to herself, *Why would they want me around when the eggs hatch. Do the little birds need a playmate?*

The blue bird with its fancy blue top-not and silver wings fluttered and flew around the nest, gaining distance between itself and Ivy. Perhaps it was afraid of her reaction when it said, *You're a large worm. You'll satisfy the babies as a tender and tasty morsel. Toodle-oo.*

Ivy decided she didn't like birds, not in the least bit. And now she had an even larger problem. She was thousands of feet in the air on a sheer cliff face waiting to be served to a bunch of hungry babies as dinner.

She was scared. There was no denying that. Ivy slowly walked around the inside of the nest, peering over the side. It was a very long way down.

Sparky? Sparky? I'm in big trouble.

A large gray bird with a cruel beak and beady eyes as big as Ivy's fist flew from a tall point where it seemed to be keeping watch, and landed on the rocks above the nest where Ivy waited. *Stop that noise or I'll throw you out of the nest.*

Ivy swallowed. The big birds heard her calling for Sparky. She said, *I'm sorry. I won't say anything more.*

See that you don't.

Ivy watched the birds come and go, and tried to figure out whether there was a guard on her. The birds swapped places when sitting the nests. Sometimes it seemed like the skies were empty while at other times they were squabbling or cawing amongst themselves. They didn't caw like a crow, though. Their voices were deeper and more menacing. Ivy couldn't believe she didn't notice before. But then, how could she have guessed when they came to save her, that she was actually being saved for dessert.

Ivy's mom used to sing the Muppet songs to her at bedtime. She knew most of the songs by heart. Now was a good time for "The Rainbow Connection".

The larger birds perked up, turning their heads and listening. Ivy continued singing through that song and then started another song. And not just in her mind. She sang out loud. All the while, she tested the edge of the nest next to the cliff face for ledges. The problem with scrambling out of the nest in a hurry was that a single mistake would be followed by a long fall and a large splat.

Ivy didn't want that to happen to her, but given the choice between baby food and falling, she figured falling would be quicker and at least she would have tried to escape.

She stopped singing after several songs. When the sun was at its highest point in the sky, the flock swept off the mountainside in a beautiful pattern that would have inspired Ivy under different circumstances. The nest of eggs was manned by a single bird. Even the little birds had flown away.

It was too convenient. Ivy knew the birds were testing her in some way. She looked out over the forest to watch them soar, swooping down over the trees. She needed to wait and figure out their patterns. The babies weren't hatched yet. That gave her some time.

Ivy was glad she hadn't started her escape at that point, for it wasn't long before one of the birds swooped in and dropped a hare into the nest, it's neck broken. A little bird showed her a picture of herself gnawing on the leg.

I don't eat raw meat.

It's tasty. Go ahead. Try it. The voice sounded like the guys on her mom's exercise video. 'One more. You can do it.'

Ivy was grossed out by the dead animal, but decided if she were going to be killed, she might as well cause some trouble of her own. They wouldn't get to eat the rabbit either. She picked it up by the scruff of the neck and pitched it over the nest, aiming just to the left of the little bird.

Startled, the little bird fluttered its feathers. The top knot wobbled once and the little bird disappeared over the side. The hare bounced along rocks and fell to a ledge fifty feet below the nest.

You're an unpleasant worm.

Ivy crossed her arms and pulled back to the side of the nest closest to the cliff. She was feeling particularly vulnerable.

Angry at the little bird, she started a song of her own, one that she made up as she went. *I like dragons who eat little birds, who toast their tails and roast their beaks. Dragons that grind birds in their teeth and use their bones to floss between.*

Ivy paused to see if there had been any movement, but it was quiet below. The little bird was there. Ivy could feel it fluttering at the tip of her mind, like a thought that she couldn't quite think of. She decided that even if no birds were listening, the song was at least making her feel better.

Little blue-birds taste like chicken. When you fry them, their wings thicken. Oh, little blue-birds. How I wish that Sparky could hear me...so that she could have a snack. A blue bird swallowed near her snout, swallowed whole but the leg sticking out. Little blue-birds.

Hey, is that song about me? The bird flew around the nest

once and landed on the edge across from Ivy. A chunk of rabbit fur was stuck to his beak, and Ivy knew at once what he had been doing.

The gray birds will be mad that little blue-bird took my food. Little blue-bird. Since I should be fat and ready to feed their young when they are old. Ivy smiled. It was ridiculous. She was about to be eaten or thrown out of a nest to fall thousands of feet and somehow the song was making her feel better.

The bird didn't seem terribly upset. He was preening his feathers and watching Ivy, waiting to hear the next line of the song.

When a blue bird flies so high, soaring in the lonesome sky, while the dragons lick their lips, little blue bird. Sparky, where are you? Little blue bird is going to feed me to the eggs. Now I fear that I'll be dead. Little Blue bird.

Ivy stopped singing, hoping to hear Sparky's voice, hoping for some advice on what to do next, but the only voice she heard was the birds. *My name is Twif. Can you put my name in the song?*

Her universe just kept getting stranger and stranger. Ivy wouldn't be surprised at anything anymore. Dreams came true, but not all dreams were good. Alien worlds were real. Dragons, too. And here was a bird who wanted his name in a song. *Twif the tweeter, sang much sweeter when I stood upon the ground. When the dragons eat Twif's tail, the little bird will taste so stale. Because he's so rouuuunnnnnnd...*Ivy took a little break from singing to tell Twif *Because you've eaten so much rabbit, you see.*

But I'm not round. Twif looked down at himself and then at Ivy. *I'm not round enough for the song.*

No, you're not. You need to eat more of that rabbit if you want to be round enough for the song.

Twif's head drooped. *But I'm already full.*

Full isn't the same thing as round. Ivy said.

With a nod, Twif launched himself from the nest and swirled in spiraling circles down fifty feet to the rabbit.

What happens to Twif next?

Well, he was eaten. I suppose he doesn't do anything.

Oh. Can't you have him save a cute little green bird, one with yellow wings and a nice smile? Maybe he can save her from the dragons.

Something about that question seemed so human. Ivy leaned her head back against the nest and sang.

Twif, the mighty. Twif, the great. Saved Ivy first and sealed his fate. For the hero found his mate. She was running, fleeing, still retreating from the scary dragon's teeth. Twif, the mighty, who saved Ivy also saved his lady love. They found a nest and put to rest all the fear of dragon kin. For the dragon, who loved Ivy, declared Twif forever friend.

Twif flew back up to the top of the nest and hopped down inside with Ivy. *Who's Ivy?*

That's me. Ivy said.

If I save you, will I be dragon friend? Twif fluttered his wings and hopped into the nest, preening his feathers and standing proudly as if it had already happened.

Well, Sparky will be your friend. She's a very nice dragon. Ivy wasn't too sure about other dragons.

I've never heard of Sparky. Is she big?

Even with her life in danger, Ivy didn't want to lie. Sparky as a newborn was certainly not a big dragon, not even medium-sized. But she was bigger than Twif and would grow bigger every day. Ivy decided to tell the truth, but make it sound good. *Well, Sparky is a bit bigger than you, but she was just born, so she has a lot of growing up to do. There's no telling how big she could get. Someday, I think she'll be dragon-sized.*

I'll save you and become dragon-friend.

Ivy watched the little bird strut across the floor of the nest with its chest puffed out and its wings whipping along the air. Twif had an active imagination, for a bird.

That's nice.

Ivy planned on escaping all right. But not with Twif. The bird was tiny for one thing and likely to be a spy for another. Ivy didn't count on Twif being such a single-minded fanatic about rescuing her.

What do we do first? Twif flew to Ivy and landed on her shoulder. So now Twif wanted to be friends, now that it suited the crazy little bird. And Ivy had no idea what to tell the bird. She couldn't tell him of her plans to escape. He might tell the larger birds in trade for being hero of the skies.

Do you know when the eggs will hatch? Ivy asked. She was getting restless with only a ten foot space to exist in. And she was getting thirsty.

Any day now. Not what Ivy was hoping to hear.

Is there a time when most of the birds are away?

In the evening we swim in the lake. We play there for a few hours and only the nest-sitters won't swim. I'll stay here with you and we can escape then.

Ivy decided that she would try it this evening. Not that she'd probably get far, but she had to try. *Perhaps we should think about this more.*

I love swimming. You don't mind if I go? I promise not to tell the others about our plans. The big birds won't let me swim every day. Ivy watched the little bird and found herself pitying the creature. Not that she could do anything to help. She had to help herself first.

But something in the way the bird followed the larger animals, making plans based solely on what the large birds said, saddened Ivy and reminded her of David teasing her every day in school. What if she didn't have friends? What if David was a monster instead of a boy and would eat her if he got angry enough? Maybe she'd follow the largest creature at a whim, too.

You go swimming. I bet the water feels cool. Which reminded Ivy how thirsty she had gotten since waking up.

Ivy and Twif talked for the rest of the day. She gathered as much information listening to Twif and watching the other birds as she could. Three birds swooped at the edges of the flock watching for predators. Ivy shuddered to think of something large enough to take down one of them.

The nesters sat on the eggs. Twif said in the early morning, they would get a quick bite to eat while their spouses sat the nests. The day would be the worst time to escape. That was when the birds slept. Ivy could see his point. The birds were all perched with their beaks tucked into their breasts snoozing.

She checked the cliff for small fissures and about thirty feet from the nest where she was trapped, Ivy thought she found a crack small enough to fit through. Her goal when the birds went to swim was to climb out of the nest and work her way to the crack, slipping inside and hiding until the next evening. Thirty feet. In ground terms, that really wasn't very far at all. But in cliff terms, Ivy thought she should have a plan to hide. And stay hidden.

During the middle of the day Ivy couldn't stand the thirst anymore. She asked Twif for a drink. *Maybe you could get me a canteen of water, so when you're flying or away, I can still have water to drink.*

Twif knew what a canteen was and without answering flew to a large gray bird with silver-white feathers and a brown speckled breast. After a quick exchange of tweets with the bird, the two flew off.

A while later, the birds flew back with a large water pouch, full of water. Ivy drank her fill. She decided she needed more time to plan her escape.

Ivy stepped to the edge of the nest and looked over. The distance to the ground was fearsome, but she forced herself to look down. It was a long, long way. And as far as it was to fall, Ivy knew she would have to climb down, inch by inch, with dangerous predators all around. Tears filled her eyes and she wiped them angrily away. Aloud she whispered, "Mrs. Huffity says I can do anything I set my mind to. And I can do this."

Ivy forced herself to look straight down, leaning over the protective wall of the nest to do it. With a sigh, she said, "Boy, am I in trouble."

The largest birds left the nests first. Soon flocks were sweeping the skies above Ivy and the worst part of watching them leave was knowing that the moment had come.

A few birds nested. Ivy would have to take the chance that they wouldn't kill her as she crawled out. Beyond the nest was a rocky ledge, and that was Ivy's first goal. The nest's edge was about as high as the counter in her kitchen, which made for a safe nest, but it was hard to climb. She put her hands on the top and hoisted herself up, putting her knee on the top just like she would at home, but at home she couldn't see a thousand tiny trees in the distance. She didn't feel brave enough to stand straight up. Instead she inched her way to the other side and lowered herself on the smooth rock. The ledge gave her just a few feet before it dropped off to a steep cliff face.

She looked at the nearest nest, but the bird was dozing. So far, none of them had made a peep. Her heart sped as she prepared for the dangerous part. One slip and she would die. With a deep breath, Ivy pushed her glasses back and stepped to the edge of the premonitory. The crack in the rock face seemed so far away now, but if she could just get there, it was the perfect fit for her and it seemed to go deep enough that Ivy could wedge herself in.

The first step went well. A little trail followed the edge of the rock-face and while it only gave her just enough space for her own body, she could hug the rock and move towards the crevice. The trail narrowed to a point along the cliff face. Ivy reached the end. She stood at the end for what felt like forever. She didn't dare look down. The crack wasn't too far away. She planned her foot holds in her mind, where she would place her hands, how she would move.

Starting was the hard part, the hardest thing she had ever done or would ever do. Finally, she stepped to the first foothold, leaning into the cliff face and grasping the small ledges with everything she had. Methodically she stepped from one foothold to the next. Her path mapped out in her mind, she could no longer see the crack or know how far by sight. She could only step to the next hold and the next.

A breeze started to blow and when Ivy reached for one of the cracks that she could grip, a shower of rocks fell past her. Shaking Ivy closed her eyes. *I can do this.* The moment passed and Ivy found a steadier place to pull herself.

The crack in the rocks opened on a thin ledge, just Ivy's size. Although the distance between that crack and the next wasn't far, by the time she stepped to the ledge, her arms and legs felt like jelly.

She inched her way along, the wind making her nose run. Her hands were shaking when she wiped her nose. When another gust of wind burst by, she turned her head hoping to avoid it. Her glasses slid down her nose and off her face. They landed at her feet, bouncing once. That bounce did it.

With a gasp, Ivy watched as her glasses fell down. She felt sick to her stomach watching the distance, realizing how very far it was and feeling the chill wind rising. She closed her eyes for a moment to catch her breath, her body hugging the rock wall. *Just a few more steps. I can make it.*

If the birds ever noticed her climbing the wall, they didn't cry out in alarm. As she stepped into the darkness of the crack, Ivy thought about the distance down the cliff face and realized how difficult it would be. Somehow she had imagined the journey to the crack would be easy. The crack dipped just a little bit below the ledge.

Now that she knew what was in store, she didn't see how she would make it all the way down the cliff face. She climbed deeper into the darkness until the crack ended and she was hidden from the birds and tucked into rock. Curling up on the cold hard surface, she decided to rest.

Somehow Ivy fell asleep on that barren slab of rock, wedged as far into the crevice as she could fit. During the night a storm blew in. Ivy awoke to wind blasting into the crack. With it came rain. She wasn't sure that the nests would feel much better in the downpour, but Ivy was feeling miserable and disheartened.

She called out to Sparky. *Sparky? Are you there?*

No Sparky. She called again.

Instead, she got Twif. A few minutes after her calls, the little bird dove into the crack. *You're here. I was looking for you.*

Ivy sat up, her back resting against the smoothest part of the crack. She felt squished. *I need Sparky. I can't climb all the way down the cliff.*

Twif fluttered down to sit on Ivy's knee. *It's not that far. You can do it.*

Ivy shivered as a freezing gust of wind blew into the crack. *It's so cold in here. I can't climb down a cliff in the rain. I'll decide what to do tomorrow.*

She really didn't know what to do. Without Sparky or

Mrs. Huffity, she was in a bind, that much was certain.

Do the others know that I'm gone?

Twif cocked his head. *The bird who brought you to the nest says he will come to get you when the eggs hatch.*

He won't be able to reach me in here. Ivy said.

You'll have to come out for food or water or to make an escape. He's not worried. Most worms that fall out of the nest die or wriggle on the ground injured for a while. Twif hopped once on Ivy's knee.

Were they like me? The ones who fell?

Yes. The same and different. All try to escape, but it's too far down.

By now the wind was howling. Twif looked outside, *I will see you in the morning. My nest is more comfortable.*

And Twif flew away. Ivy wasn't surprised. The bird seemed to do whatever it felt like doing without regard to anyone else. But she felt lonely without him there. And scared. She didn't want to die of starvation or thirst in this crack.

And that's when she realized that she was wasting an opportunity to gather drinking water. Taking the canteen that Twif gave her, she held it at the angle the rain was blowing. She was already soaked and shivering, but at least now she would have something to drink. Ivy longed most of all for a warm bed and the furnace.

The night was endless. Ivy thought she might have fallen asleep once, but if she did she was immediately awake again because of the driving rain and the sound of the wind. Nothing was going right, and she wondered how she could ever escape. As she huddled between two cold, wet rocks, she wondered whether Carrie knew she was missing and if Carrie was talking to her parents right now. Maybe Carrie was in this world, too, facing a scary skeleton. Ivy was beginning to think any fate was better than hers.

Chapter 14

Meanwhile, Carrie taught the princess how to be a friend. It was a long process, mostly because for years, the princess lorded over everyone around her. Carrie wouldn't let her use her royalty as an excuse to act spoiled.

They sat on the bed in Carrie's bedchamber where earlier they had been jumping, and Carrie told Minerva about the egg and all of the strange happenings at her school.

"Why don't you just have a tutor? Mother says that only the poor go to classrooms with other children." They were sitting in chairs before a roaring fire. Minerva described how the smoke was sent through several tunnels up to the air so they didn't get sick.

"I'm not exactly poor, but we're not as rich as you. Not many people have tutors." Carrie stretched out letting her toes warm in the heat. Had she known of Ivy's plight at that very moment, she would have felt guilty that she was so comfortable, but Carrie was happy. Her troubles seemed so far away when she was in this underground world.

"Will you marry someone my father chooses?" The princess asked.

"I'm much too young to marry." Carrie said.

The princess didn't sound convinced when she said, "Me, too."

"Do they still want me to marry someone from here?" Carrie thought she'd talked the king out of it.

"In time...when you're old enough."

"But why? I'm a commoner." Carrie didn't say it with anger or frustration, just curiosity. She didn't care that she was a commoner. She had been one all her life.

Minerva shrugged, "It's the way of things. You rescued a princess, so you will get rewarded with royal marriage."

Carrie grabbed the fire poker and pushed the logs around until the fire grew bright again. "That's so middle ages. I live in the modern world."

"But my father planned so carefully for my capture and subsequent rescue. It was a great disappointment when things went so awry." Princess Minerva sat at the edge of her chair. "You don't have to do that. We have servants."

"I like poking at it." Carrie said, "Haven't you ever done it before?"

Minerva giggled, "My mom would kill me. Here, let me try." The princess awkwardly pushed around a log, squealing when sparks flew and laughing when she managed to entice a twig into flame. She wore a blue gown that shimmered in the glow of the fire.

Carrie decided to get serious. "Minerva, I have to go home. I really appreciate everything your family has done for me, but my parents will worry."

The princess rested the poker on the grate, sitting silently for so long Carrie wasn't even sure that she'd been heard. Finally, Minerva said, "You can't. I'm sorry, but my father instructed the guards to keep you here and if you leave the grounds to bring you back here when you were done."

"Done with what?"

"Shopping. The clothes you were wearing..." The princess looked uncomfortable.

"It's okay. You can say it. My clothes are terrible. They are what we sleep in where I come from. They're not to be seen in public." Carrie ran to the bed and knelt down, grabbing her pajama tops and carried them back to the princess. While the clothes the princess let her borrow were nice, the pajamas were even better. "Feel the fabric."

The princess stroked the fleece. "It's so soft."

"It's not meant to be worn outside. I'm afraid they're ruined now. I've been running outside in them and kept in that cage. They're dirty and they're meant to be indoor clothes."

"I'll have one of the maids wash it for you. It's softer than the cloth the best spinners and weavers make. Do you think we could travel to your village and buy some?" Minerva held the fabric between her finger and thumb. "It's thick. I bet it's warm."

"Yes. Do you know how to travel between worlds? We could buy pajamas there, but I don't know how to get home."

"I can't go through the gates. It's forbidden."

Carrie looked up, "So you know a way out of this world?"

"Sure. Everyone does. Overworld and Underworld. We have to watch for strangers and be careful that no one crosses accidentally."

Carrie kicked at the fire grate. "What happens if you break the rule? I mean, you're the princess, so how would you be punished?"

Minerva lifted her head with a gleam in her eye. "You're right. And I do love those pajamas. We'll bring enough back for the whole family."

"Shall we go now?" Carrie asked.

"It's a long way to the gates. We should sleep first and go in daylight."

Minerva and Carrie spent a long time in front of the fire talking and planning. More than once the room rang with laughter, and Carrie was grateful that she found a new friend in this strange world.

Chapter 15

Ivy sneezed, her nose stuffed from hiding all night in wet clothes. Her throat felt scratchy, but worse, she couldn't get warm. She just kept shivering. The sun was out now and the birds were awake. They cried out as they circled above the crack. Ivy thought she had gone unnoticed until one of the large gray birds flew to the ledge and landed where the crack began.

While confident that the bird wouldn't be able to reach her, Ivy scooted back further against the rock face hoping the bird wouldn't notice her. When a large eye appeared at the crack, Ivy scrunched further back and held completely still.

The bird's body was too large for the crack, but their heads were somewhat smaller. Ivy hit her head against the rock when the bird pushed it's head into the crack, the beak opening and closing as if to capture Ivy and crush her. She jumped up. The beak scraped against her shoe.

Sparky! Twif! Somebody help! Ivy jumped again when the beak shifted forward, trying to capture her.

Watching the bird stretch its neck, Ivy had an idea. It wasn't a very grand idea, and she wondered if she'd even live to regret it. Ivy jumped up where the two rock walls met and climbed up by stretching her legs out so that she was in between the two walls the way she and Carrie climbed the hallway at Carrie's house. When the bird shifted its weight to get its head deeper in the hole and look up, Ivy dropped on its neck.

She felt like an alligator wrestler. She'd seen it once on reality television. She knew if she let go, the bird would hurt her, so she held onto its neck with all her might even while the bird thrashed back and forth banging Ivy against the rocks.

The secret to Ivy's grip was in her legs. Although her arms were wrapped tightly around the bird, it was her legs that the bird couldn't shake. She locked them at the ankles and didn't care much if the bird choked to death.

Little worm. What are you doing? The big one will punish you. Twif swooped into the crack and fluttered in a tight circle around Ivy, unwilling to land.

I'm not a worm. And you had better tell your friend here to fly me back to the ground far away from any of these nests or any other birds. If he takes me anywhere dangerous I will strangle him. And I

don't care how hard it is for him to fly, I'm not letting go until I'm safe.
Ivy shook with fatigue and adrenaline. Holding on was easier
with her limbs locked. The pressure it would take for the
bird to remove her was more than it had. She wasn't sure
what would happen when they landed but she had the feeling
if she let go now, all of her options would be gone.

No doubt the bird would peck her to death, but she
was in an impossible situation now, freezing cold, hungry,
tired, and utterly alone. She couldn't count Twif as a friend
or an ally. Yes, she was alone. Ivy took a deep breath as tears
filled her eyes. She had to keep her head.

Twif exchanged chatter with the bird and then told
Ivy, *He agrees. He's taking you now.*

The bird swung its head back, perhaps hoping to
catch Ivy off guard, but she clung to the bird because she
knew her life depended on it. Curling in so that her head was
under her shoulders, she could smell the bird's neck. It was
an animal smell, not distasteful, just different. She didn't
open her eyes as the bird pushed off from the cliff.

Twif, what do I do when he lands? He will try to eat me.

She couldn't see Twif, but could imagine him
swooping in excited spirals around the big bird. She heard
Twif's voice in her head. *The big birds don't like the blackberry*

patches. Find a tall one and he can push you inside and then you can let him go. You'll have to run deeper in, but at least you'll have a chance.

Will you come with me into the blackberries? Ivy asked.

Yes. I will help you find the dragons. Twif certainly was stuck on dragons.

Give the bird instructions on where to land, and you can travel with me to find the dragons. Ivy clung to the bird with everything she had. Her hands shook. Were it not for her legs locked around the bird's neck, she would have fallen right at the start. The bird was turning an odd shade of purple. Ivy kept clinging.

They never reached the blackberries. The bird started to lose consciousness. Realizing what was happening, it swooped down in an attempt to save its own life and completely blacked out ten feet from the ground.

Ivy and the bird tumbled through a field of grass. Her ankles were locked firmly around the bird's neck and while she lay with her arm across the bird's eyes, she couldn't seem to move.

Are you hurt? Twif swooped down and landed on a stump.

I'm fine. I'm just having trouble untangling myself. Ivy was still shivering when she managed to pull her leg out from underneath the bird's neck.

You'd better hurry before Striker wakes up.

The name *Striker* was enough motivation for Ivy to untangle herself completely and stumble away.

Where do I go? Are the others after me? Ivy scanned the skies. Although several of the same kind of birds were in the air, none of them seemed the least bit interested in her. Not yet. When they realized she had escaped...that would be a different matter.

There's a nice little hidey-hole at the end of the field. You can burrow in and get warm.

The idea of burrowing into dirt did not appeal to Ivy. She told Twif. *I'm not a burrowing kind of animal. Aren't there any houses nearby?*

There's the castle on the other side of the mountains. You could go there. But first we need to get away from Striker. Twif pushed off the stump and flew in a circle around Ivy. Shivering, she followed his lead. Although her legs didn't feel much like moving, she ran across the field, putting as much distance as she could between herself and the bird. She turned back once to see the large head rising and looking around as if dazed. She ran faster.

In here. Just for the night.

Ivy climbed into the hole and discovered that the hole opened into a cavern with a rock floor. She went further in and discovered a lattice of caves. From the entrance Twif called, *Worm? Worm? Can you come back?*

Ivy gritted her teeth. *Would you quit calling me Worm? My name is Ivy. And you can come in here with me. There's plenty of room.*

I'm sorry. I'll call you Ivy now. I'm afraid of the hidey-holes. Your kind eat birds. We can't escape in under-the-sky places. Ivy couldn't exactly deny it, although the chickens she ate never talked back to her. Of course, most of the farmers she grew up around raised cattle and sheep, not chickens.

Just come in. I'm going further and if you want to meet a dragon, you have to go where I go. It's not like I enjoyed being a thousand feet in the air either. Ivy waited in the twilight darkness for a long time. She thought maybe Twif had flown away. She was cold, tired, hungry, and angry. Somehow she ended up dumped on this strange world without a friend or any way to get home. At least three different kinds of creatures had tried to kill her. It put her in no mood to negotiate with Twif who had originally helped the big birds catch Ivy.

The bird flew in, swooping low and landing on Ivy's shoulder. Twif held his wings tight to his body and said, *I don't like this.*

Neither do I, but I don't have much choice.

The hidey-hole Ivy had climbed in was the skylight of a network of caves. She could see another skylight ahead, a natural opening in the top of a cave made from an opening in the ground. But the dangers made themselves all too clear when she banged her head on a sharp, low ceiling. A trickle of warm blood poured down the side of her head. "Tigers and Catnip." She said out loud. It was her mother's swear word when things were really bad, and seemed appropriate for the moment.

You're dripping on me. Twif complained.

I know. I'm sorry. Her clothes had never completely dried and Ivy was so demoralized that it seemed impossible to go on. *Twif, do you think we're safe here? Will the larger birds poke their head in to grab us?*

I don't know. Twif jerked his wing away in agitation when another drop of Ivy's blood dripped on him. *I need a bath. And I don't like it here.*

Without another word, Twif launched from her shoulder and straight out the sky light. Ivy, feeling abandoned, decided that she would move just a little deeper into the caves. She took each step carefully, not trusting the dim light coming through the hole in the cavern roofs.

She traveled into the darkness until she could only see the dimmest light from the skylight behind her. Then sinking to the ground, she gave in to sleep, her body so cold it had given up shivering.

Chapter 16

Twif dunked his wings a few times in the lake,
whistling a little bird tune. Once he was clean, he jetted
directly back to the skylight where he'd left Ivy, only to find
that she was gone. *Ivy? Where are you?*

He hopped into the hole and for a moment it felt as if
the sides of the cavern were moving to crush him. Shutting
his eyes he stayed in that patch of light. *I'm friend of the dragon,
and nothing can hurt me. Ivy? Are you there?*

He felt her nearby. There was no way to describe the
sensation, for it was a bird's feeling unique to birds and
unknown by anyone else, but he felt Ivy and knew she was
close and even knew what direction she went.

He hopped ever so carefully into the dark. *Snakes.
Weasels. They all live underground with the worms. Helloooo? Ivy?
Please answer. I know you're hiding from me. I'm sorry I left.*

Having drippy flesh on his wing was gross. He liked to
be clean and always bathed after eating or when he got dirty.

He hopped a little further into the darkness and realized that Ivy was right there after all. She'd only gone far enough into the darkness to hide, but she was asleep. Twif figured that he would sleep, too. He perched on her ankle because nothing down there was leaking and tucked his head into his wing and fell asleep.

It was not a weasel or a snake that disturbed Twif, but the dark worms, the ones who lived all day under the earth and seemed like transparent copies of their above-world counterparts. He hopped away, abandoning Ivy. His mind knew only to run and didn't consider whether he liked Ivy, how much he liked Ivy, or even whether it mattered if she was captured. He only knew to run.

He perched in the dark while the men discovered her.

"Poor lass. Looks like she knocked herself out cold. Comes from above, this one."

"Your wife could use another foundling to care for. Maybe she won't cry so much at night."

Marilee Jenns was a mother to all of the children of the underworld, baking them treats, bandaging their cuts and scrapes, but her own hurt went deep. She couldn't have her own children and took in strays. Her husband catered to her deep need to mother. And so, he took Ivy home with him deep into the caves.

Twif followed close behind, gliding and flapping and hoping he didn't run into a wall. The deeper he went the worse he felt. A bird wasn't meant for underground. He grew uneasy as the road turned steeper and the darkness became unbearable. He would have turned around, but by then he'd lost his way. He hoped the dragon would like him. That would make it all worthwhile.

$$* * *$$

When Ivy awoke, she was in an oversized nightgown lying on a strange bed. The bed was fluffy and comfortable and built onto a stone ledge. For a minute, she thought she was back with the birds, but a soft lantern in the dark and the black rock wall told her that she was safe.

Rolling onto her side, Ivy pulled the blankets to her shoulder and closed her eyes for a few more minutes before sneezing. Her throat had the tickle that comes before a sore throat. But she wasn't cold anymore.

Hearing her sneeze, Merilee said, "Oh, you're awake. What a darling. Are you feeling better?"

Ivy didn't really feel much like talking, but she had to

be polite. After all, this woman had probably saved her life. "Much better, thank you."

"Does your head hurt?" Merilee came into the light and Ivy had a bit of a start. Fortunately, she'd seen these skeleton folk in her dreams. Merilee was a heavy-set woman with large arms and an ample body, but that bulk was translucent and behind the bulk, Ivy could see a skeleton. It reminded her of one of the fishes she had seen on television.

Ivy's head did ache. So much that she didn't even bother to turn when Merilee sat back down, out of sight. "Yes. Have you been sitting with me?"

"A head injury can be dangerous. I've woken you up twice." Merilee's voice was as warm as honey, soothing and sweet, and Ivy immediately liked her.

"I don't remember." Ivy felt so tired, her eyelids drooped. If she could just keep them open a minute longer. It was rude to fall asleep talking. But Ivy couldn't help it. She fell asleep to Merilee's sing-song voice telling her that everything would be okay.

While Ivy slept, Merilee said to Twif, "You might as well come in. This one will be asleep for hours more. She'll have the sniffles for a week."

Twif flew in and perched on a crease in the blankets.

He didn't bother talking to Merilee. She was a creature of the underground. He'd stay awake until Ivy could keep watch for him. He didn't want to end up in a bowl of soup this close to being named dragon-friend.

Ivy woke up scared. This time she didn't have dreams about Carrie underground or Sparky high on a mountain. She dreamed that the birds kept pecking her. She cried out with her hands on her head. Marilee touched Ivy's hair softly and told her that it was just a dream.

Her head still hurt, but this time she wanted to get up. "Is it okay if I walk around a little?" Ivy asked. She felt like a giant toad had landed on her chest and stayed there. She could still breathe, but she needed to move.

"Of course. Let me get my basket and we can visit Florence. You'll like her." Merilee bustled across the room to a cupboard with a wooden door fitted deftly into the stone. "There have been a number of strangers in the halls lately. It wouldn't do for you to be walking alone."

"Was there another little girl like me?" Ivy asked. "I'm looking for my friend, Carrie."

Merilee hugged Ivy's shoulder, "I'm sure we'll find someone your age to play with, Dear. But the only other girl found in the tunnels was the princess's friend. We won't see her."

"I think it's Carrie. Maybe you can just send a message from me and ask?"

They were in the halls now and Merilee shushed her kindly. "One does not ask for an audience with the king. It just isn't done."

She'd never had to deal with kings before, but from her own experience at school, Ivy figured the king was probably a bit like the principal. Not there every day, unless you caused problems or did something really extraordinary. Except for good grades, Ivy was average. She didn't win the best poster or poem contests, so as far as the principal was concerned, she was just a name on the roster.

"If I caused a lot of problems, would I have to go before the king to be sentenced?" Ivy asked.

Twif made a phft noise from Ivy's shoulder. Merilee laughed, "Your friend has the right of it. You don't want to do anything bad enough to get the king's attention."

They turned down a tunnel. Merilee was kind enough to give Ivy a little light to carry so that she could easily see her way through. "Come along. Florence will ask you a thousand questions about the overworld. I think she secretly wants to move into the sunlit countries but is too afraid to take the first step."

Merilee rang a little bell outside a slatted door that seemed hung from the ceiling. It was then that they heard the screams.

Chapter 17

Carrie and the princess lounged in front of the fire, a favorite place because as the princess explained, only the very privileged were allowed flame under the world. It was too expensive to remove the smoke. The underground tunnels always tended toward cool and Carrie was used to an indoor temperature that was much warmer.

"I have to go home, back to the overworld." Carrie said. "I like it here, but my family will worry."

"Stay right here." Minerva stood and with careful and precise steps left the room. Any other kid would go dashing out. Not Minerva. But at least they jumped on the bed. And Minerva spoke to Carrie like a friend.

Minerva returned and sat primly back in her chair. Handing Carrie a bracelet, she said, "This is a portal to our world. My father bought three from the portal guardians. He gave me one and is holding the other ones. He's afraid I'll lose it."

That sounded more like a regular father to Carrie. "What do I do?"

"If you're in the other world and want to come here, put on the bracelet. See that little ruby stone there?" The princess pointed to a glittering red stone set between two yellow stones. "Just touch that red stone on the front at the same time that you touch the yellow stone here on the side. You have to think really hard that you want to use the bracelet and where you want to be. It's smart so you won't accidentally end up traveling when you don't want to."

Carrie took the bracelet from Minerva carefully. The bracelet was beautiful with many sparkling colors that glowed in the firelight. "Thank you."

"Would it bring me to my world?" Carrie wanted to put the bracelet on right then and try it. But she didn't want to seem rude.

"You can try it out if you want." Minerva said. "The world you came from belongs to the yellow stones."

Carrie tried it on and then pressed the yellow stones while thinking hard of her room. Nothing happened.

"It's still a beautiful bracelet," she said, disappointed.

"It works." Minerva said, "When you want to come here, it will work."

Carrie left the bracelet on and changed the subject to the places they'd seen. Carrie started telling Minerva about camping. She was explaining to Minerva what marshmallows were and how to cook them over a fire when a loud screeching sound echoed through the roof.

"We have to go." Minerva stared at the fire while black soot and ash shook loose from the hole above and fell onto the flames.

"What is it?" Carrie leaned over the fire and twisted her head to look up, but the hole was dark.

"Don't. They're coming." Grabbing Carrie's hand, Minerva tugged her until Carrie was running behind her in and out of halls. Everyone else had the same thing in mind. It seemed everyone in the underground gathered in the halls which were getting congested.

One of the guards saw Minerva and started pushing people aside, yelling, "Make way. Make way for the princess."

Carrie heard a scream and then a surge in the crowd made people cram together as they ran through the halls. Once a woman in front of her stumbled, and Carrie felt the crowd behind her when she tried to stop herself. With one hand on the wall, she helped the woman up, thinking of the stories of people who were trampled.

The crowd pressed until Carrie felt claustrophobic and wondered if she would suffocate in the mass of people. She had lost sight of Minerva who had followed the guard without hesitation even when the woman beside her fell. Carrie had stopped and turned and now she was alone in the crowd. While the people around her seemed to see in the dark, Carrie could only make out the shadowy forms of people in the dim light while she struggled to follow the masses.

The hall opened to a large cavern. Sunlight filtered in from the roof, and plants grew on the ledges of the high rock walls. The room was filling with people, although it seemed that the cavern still had lots of space. She found the princess standing with a pair of guards high on the wall, out of the way of the crowds. If Carrie was right, King Glome was seated on a throne near where the princess stood.

It seemed like a good time to escape. She wanted to know first what was going on. If all of the underground dwellers ran for this cavern, then Carrie was willing to bet there was something outside the cavern that was scary or dangerous or both.

Minerva was searching the cavern for Carrie. From

the place where Carrie waited, she could see the princess searching the crowd looking back and forth. Sinking back behind a large rock, Carrie sat down. She felt rude for hiding. She liked Minerva after the rocky start they had, but she needed to regroup.

She watched the people coming in. Many of them were dressed in work clothes. Now that she could see, the difference between the working class and royalty was apparent.

"Are you an overworlder?" A girl a few years younger than Carrie crept from her mother's side to take a seat next to Carrie.

"Yes." Carrie whispered. She didn't want to draw a lot of attention to herself. As the only overworlder in the room, it wouldn't take long for the princess to find her once she started asking others to look.

"Why are you here?"

"It's a long story." One that Carrie really, seriously, did NOT want to tell.

"There's another overworlder girl here, too. She's staying down the hall with Mama Merilee. Her name is Ivy. She has a funny bird."

For the first time since Carrie went underground, she had hope. "Ivy? She's my best friend. Do you know where she is?"

The little girl grinned. It was a little disconcerting to see the length of the teeth above her nearly invisible lips. "Sure. Follow me."

Carrie had settled behind a boulder along the wall. Now she was darting and weaving among the folk milling about waiting for an explanation about what just happened. The cave was brighter than the tunnels and Carrie let out a whoop when she saw Ivy.

The friends hugged while nearby underworlders looked on with amusement.

"You're here." Carrie leaned in close and whispered, "You would not believe what I have been through."

Ivy laughed, "I think I would."

A trumpet, just loud enough to get everyone's attention rang out from the front of the cavern. One of the generals, a tall distinguished gentleman in a long red overcoat stood on the raised rock that formed a natural dais.

"The men will be going out soon to face the enemy." The crowd roared in approval. Ivy pulled Carrie back into the tunnels, away from the people and waved to Merrilee to tell her everything was okay. Twif followed.

"I'm so glad you're here. How do we get home?" Carrie allowed herself to be dragged into the dark hallways.

"I have no idea. Mrs. Huffity brought me here, and we rescued Sparky and then there was a fight. I don't know what happened." Ivy and Carrie slipped into the dark corridor.

Twif fluttered. *I don't like it in the dark. Can't we go back?*

Twif, can you find the surface? Do you have the ability to find the sky and lead us out of here?

Yes, I think so. I smell daylight a few miles north. Twif landed on Ivy's shoulder.

Ivy petted Twif's head. She was growing fond of the little bird. *Please, lead us to daylight.*

Carrie heard Twif, too. She gasped. "Is that the bird talking to us, the way Sparky did?"

"I know. Isn't it awesome? He's going to help us get out of here." Ivy trailed a finger along the darkness of the wall. Her eyes had adjusted to the darkness. Everything was blurry without her glasses anyway.

"We'd better hurry. I don't know what the trouble is, but I was locked in a cage and only escaped by coming down here. We need to find Sparky and get out of here."

Twif gave Ivy directions, sometimes flying forward and back through the tunnels to make sure he was going toward the surface. They heard rumbling behind them and the sounds of clashing metal.

"Looks like it's already happening." Carrie said, with a glance behind her. "I hope Minerva is okay."

"Is there anything we can do to help?" Ivy asked.

"No. Minerva said the guards would protect them. She said they would wait in the cavern until the fighting was done." Carrie frowned, "Which means we probably picked a bad time to come through the tunnels. We'd better get out now."

Twif understood what Carrie was saying and the girls started running. In the dark corridors, they ran into walls, banging their arms, knees, and foreheads a few times. "Watch out for that step." Carrie said, as she caught her foot.

"Twif says we can go up now." Ivy rubbed her arm. "My arm still hurts."

"Ask him to go ahead and see who's up there. I don't want to be captured again." Carrie took the second step and then the third. She didn't want to be stuck in the darkness, but stepping into a trap would be much worse.

Ivy blew out a huge sigh, "And we don't want to get

eaten either."

"I'm afraid to ask." Carrie yawned and stretched. "Boy, I could use some sleep."

"I've been sleeping for a day and a half."

Twif called back and the girls hurried up the stairs, the stones ringing under their feet. The stairs opened to a tower. The stones were huge. Each individual stone as tall as the girls.

"I wouldn't want to meet the builders." Ivy said.

"Sunlight at last!" Carrie did a happy dance.

Twif flew outside, but his thoughts were scattered, and he seemed to be twittering in bird song.

Ivy laughed and looked down at her ripped jeans and torn shirt. Merilee had cleaned them as much as possible, but they still looked bad. "Mom's going to kill me. I didn't realize how bad these were. Let's get going."

Carrie laughed, "I'm just happy to see light. Those tunnels are depressing."

The two girls found the exit and walked out of the stone castle onto a hillside with twisted and gnarled pines and huge boulders lying as if plucked by a giant and randomly dropped in the barren fields. "Guess it's winter here, too. I wish I had my jacket." Carrie said. "Hope it doesn't get cold. It's actually pretty nice for being this high up."

"Me too. Maybe both of us calling for Sparky and Mrs. Huffity will help. I have no idea how to get home. Some rescue this turned out to be." Ivy laughed and flipped her hair back.

"Hey, you're not wearing your glasses." Carrie exclaimed.

"Nope. They're sitting at the bottom of a very tall cliff and I have no intention of going back for them no matter how many weeks of dishes I have to wash." Ivy crossed her arms. "You know, a part of me wishes we could stay here. No school. No chores."

"Yeah...it would be fun for a while. But they don't have ice-cream here or chocolate cake, and I know my parents are a pain and my mom is acting crazy right now, but I kinda miss her."

"Me, too. But I don't get junk food anyway." Ivy said. Still, she felt homesick. Her dad would be building up a fire right now and telling her they'd get her new glasses when they returned to civilization.

Twif who soared in a circle above Ivy, asked about ice-cream and was given a long and vivid description of ice-cream with caramel and crunchy chocolate and all things delicious. He winged away with promises to return soon. All that talk of treats had made him hungry.

As they trudged down the hill, Ivy said, "I'm scared, Carrie."

"That Sparky won't answer?"

"Yeah, I mean, what if we're stuck here forever?" Ivy's green eyes were wide, and without her glasses, she seemed a lot younger.

"Okay. I'm calling her now. You do it, too. If they answer, they answer. If not, well, at least we know where we stand." Carrie closed her eyes. She had no idea how this telepathic thing worked. If she knew how to scream with her mind, she'd do it. She imagined herself with a loud and booming voice and called again and again. *Mrs. Huffity. Sparky. Mrs. Huffity.*

Ivy called to Mrs. Huffity and Sparky the way she always did, calling them by name and asking if they were there.

A quiet voice answered from a great distance. *We're here. But we have traveled a long way, and Sparky is molting. You will both need to return to the gate alone.*

We don't know how to get there. Carrie said.

Mrs. Huffity sent an image to Carrie and Ivy. It was amazing that she could send the landscape exactly as it looked. She showed them both the canyons and a river with three waterfalls. After following the river to the third waterfall, they were to turn and walk up the hillside.

Ivy opened her eyes, her mouth open. "Whoa."

"That's going to be a long walk."

It was an incredibly long walk. They were almost at the gate when both Ivy and Carrie felt a spasm of pain from Sparky, quickly covered up.

"Did you feel that?" Carrie was so sore even her arms hurt. She wanted to sleep for a year and find a nice civilized place where she could have hot baths and play computer games.

"Sparky's in trouble. I don't think she wanted us to know." Ivy looked longingly at the gate. "We can actually see it. We're almost there."

A shimmering in the air where the mist of a waterfall met sunlight made Carrie think of unicorns and magic.

"We can't go home yet, can we?" Carrie said.

"We can. I'm just not sure we should." Ivy and Carrie stopped short of the mist.

"I would really like to get out of this princess outfit."

Although Carrie had to admit, the dress was pretty and the shoes much more comfortable than any overworld dress shoes. Truly, they were more like padded slippers, like ballerina shoes, but large enough to actually feel comfortable moving in.

"And my backup pair of glasses." Ivy rubbed her eyes.

"We might not be able to get back, once we leave." Carrie thought she might stay, but Ivy had two parents who loved her more than anything. Carrie figured hardly anyone would even notice her gone, but the same was not true for her friend.

"We can't leave Sparky alone here." Ivy said.

"You should go back. Your mom will be worried." Carrie tried to be brave, tried to pretend that she could do it alone, but secretly she missed Ivy and hoped she'd have company.

"So will yours." Ivy flopped down on the ground. Until they decided finally that they were going to go home or save Sparky, she didn't want to accidentally stumble into the gate and end up back home.

"Maybe. What do you think is wrong with Sparky? She was afraid."

"Her thoughts were jumbled. I think she was trying to

hide it from us." Ivy said.

"How will we find her?"

"Find who?" Twif alighted on Ivy's shoulder.

"We've decided to find Sparky instead of going directly home." Carrie said, wanting to stick a finger out to Twif. For some reason, the bird only responded to Ivy. If Carrie got too close, Twif would fly away without explanation.

"We'll need to go north." Twif fluttered his wings and a small feather drifted down to land on Ivy's back.

"Wait. How do you know where to go?" Carrie asked.

"The dragons are loud. They hurt my ears."

"I thought you couldn't hear them." Ivy said.

Twif looked down at his feet and then cocked his head, "Maybe I hear them."

"Great. We're going to be led on a dangerous journey into unknown territory by a lying bird." Carrie threw herself onto the ground and dangled her feet over the edge.

"I want to find Sparky." Ivy said, even while she looked longingly toward the mist.

"If we leave this world, we might never get back. But then if we leave the gate, we might never go home again." Carrie leaned back and put her face up, feeling the cold speckles of mist fall on her skin. "You know, I kind of like it here."

"Wouldn't you miss your parents?" Ivy asked.

"Yes. Sometimes I'm really homesick. I just like that there is something more than my boring life." Carrie said. She pushed herself up, "Shall we go?"

Ivy nodded, "I have a feeling we're going to regret this. Twif, lead the way and don't forget how to get back to this waterfall."

"That's for sure." Carrie giggled. It might not have been the appropriate time for a laugh, but something in choosing the adventure for herself made it seem great. "I wish our phones worked out here. We could call and tell our parents we are stuck in a parallel universe and won't be home for breakfast...or dinner. I wonder what time it is there."

"No idea. Only that I think staying might actually be an improvement to the trouble we'll be in when we finally do go home." Ivy hugged Carrie, "I'm glad you're here."

But they didn't get far. Before they could leave the misty valley, Mrs. Huffity broke into their minds with her stern teacher voice. *Sparky is fine. You two get home, right now. I'll see you back at school.*

Ivy and Carrie exchanged the glance they used when

they narrowly escaped from getting into trouble. Ivy shrugged, "Guess we better head home after all."

"Yeah." Carrie sighed. "I was kind of enjoying this place once *you* got here."

"Me, too, but I'm ready for home and food and my own bed." Ivy looked up the rock face of the waterfall and then scanned the skies for Twif. "Twif? Twif! Change of plans."

The little bird circled back and swooped in front of the girls. *Here I am.*

Twif, we need to say goodbye now. We're not going to see Sparky. Mrs. Huffity said we had to go home. Ivy watched Twif circle above and remembered her promise. *Mrs. Huffity. I made a promise to Twif.*

Mrs. Huffity answered back, *Tell him to wing his way here.*

Twif heard the dragon and said, *Thank you.* Dipping a wing as a final good bye, the bird flapped into the sky.

The girls edged their way along the cliff above the waterfall. The drop was only about ten feet, and they had plenty of room while they were stepping sideways across the slippery rock.

Carrie went through first. One minute she was sprayed with the light droplets of water that mist up around waterfalls, and the next she was standing in the snow shivering. She took another step forward, only to be knocked down when Ivy came running through.

"Ommmph." Ivy fell, hitting her chin against Carrie's shoulder.

"Ow. In a hurry?" Carrie wasn't often snarky with Ivy, but her shoulder hurt.

"Sorry. I didn't want to be left behind. You just disappeared."

"What time do you think it is?" They were in the empty lot between the furniture store and the bank.

"I don't even know what day it is." Ivy said. "Let's get home before anyone sees us like this. We're a mess."

Carrie looked down and nodded. Her yellow princess slippers were splattered with all shades of brown mud, and the dress was dirty, not to mention completely out of style for a small town...or a big town. Kids just didn't wear stuff like that.

"Your house or mine?" Carrie asked. There was no question that they were going together. Both sets of parents would be angry. They might as well take them on at the same time.

"Yours?" Ivy asked, a grimace on her face. She

looked different without her glasses.

The empty lot they had magicked their way into was on Main Street and the time was late, in the middle of the night judging by the emptiness. In small towns, you might get a car traveling through once every twenty minutes, less in winter.

The air tasted different. That was the first thing Ivy noticed. Earth had a smell that was well, unique to Earth. Winter tasted like frozen water when a kid breathed.

They trudged the mile to Carrie's house. Her dad's car was in the driveway and an unknown car had been parked on the street. "Hey, my dad's there. It's a miracle."

Ivy hesitated on the threshold when Carrie opened the door. It looked like her family had guests. It wasn't the best time in the world to be crashing a party. They didn't even know what time it was.

"You're home!"

Ivy realized at that moment the kind of trouble they were in. This wasn't talking in class trouble or even forgetting your homework...this was the serious grounded for life kind. When Carrie's dad said, "You'd better call Ivy's parents. I'll call the police and let them know the girls are safe."

Police? Ooohhhh...that is not good.

That's what Ivy was thinking. And when she finished thinking the thought, she heard Twif ask *What are police?*

And then Ivy thought. *This is REALLY not good.*

But she couldn't explain to Twif or even figure out how the heck Twif was talking in her head now that she was home. Because everyone was hovering. Carrie's mom and dad and what looked like grandparents, an uncle and cousins.

Carrie was busy being hugged. Her mom sobbed with huge breaths. "Where did you go? Why didn't you call?"

Carrie's dad was busy explaining that the girls were safe at home and no, sir, no idea where they've been or what they've been up to, they just came through the door. He hung up and proceeded to call Ivy's parents.

Ivy cringed listening in to *that* phone call. She overheard her dad crying. Her dad did NOT cry EVER. It was totally weird, perhaps not like hanging out three thousand feet above the ground in a bird's nest, but weird enough.

"Yes, she's here. I'd be happy to give her a ride over."

Carrie was just pulling away from her mom when she overheard. She really wanted to talk to her dad. She said, "Ivy, want me to go with you?"

Her dad would hear nothing of Carrie going out again. He said firmly, "You get upstairs and get to bed. We'll talk about what you were doing first thing tomorrow, but you're certainly not going anywhere else tonight. And if I catch you sneaking out of the house again, you'll lose access to so many electronic devices, you'll feel stuck in the dark ages."

"Doug, she just got home..."

Carrie could see her dad's eyes squinting and his jaw harden. He was just about ready to start crabbing at her mom. And she'd nag him. And then Carrie would end up crying in her room wondering why the world hated her.

"Hey!" Carrie said. She was actually a little proud of herself. She didn't usually get in the middle of her parents' fights. Using a princess's proper mode of speaking with head tilted just so, she said, "Dad, you're always gone and sometimes I just want to talk to you. At the moment, I am tired and going to bed."

She didn't storm. She walked with her head held high, princess style. After all princesses didn't need to cause a scene or slam their doors. They knew when they spoke someone would listen. It worked for Minerva. It would work for Carrie.

Carrie's dad stopped talking in mid-sentence. He

watched Carrie walk up the stairs. Shaking his head, he said, "We'd better get going." From the top of the stairs, Carrie paused and listened, wishing he would apologize to Mom, but he didn't, and she didn't either.

Her mom stood silently looking everywhere but at her estranged husband. The rest of the family chattered noisily, wondering out loud where the girls had been.

* * *

Ivy pulled the seatbelt across her lap and watched while Carrie's dad turned on the car. Feeling particularly brave, Ivy said, "Are you and your wife going to get together again?"

Grumbling a bit, he said, "Not last I checked. Did Carrie put you up to this?"

"No. I'm just wondering how much damage control I'll have to do next time I see her. You know, she saw your car here and thought it was a miracle. I don't understand why you can't just talk it out. That's what you tell me and Carrie to do when we get into a fight." Ivy wouldn't have long to talk. They were already halfway to her house. The drive was only five minutes. She'd never actually talked to an adult the way she talked to Carrie. She felt brave and a little sick to her stomach all at once.

"Look, it's complicated adult stuff. We're not getting back together. That kid you don't like, David? Are you ever going to talk it out with him? I mean to a point where you'd want to spend a lot of time with him."

Ivy groaned, "No way."

"Well, that's the way I feel. So where were you and Carrie?"

Whoa. Now that's quite a change of subject. Ivy had no idea what to say. He had the father look on his face, one she'd be getting any time now from her own father. Finally she sighed and said, "It's complicated kid stuff."

No one was more surprised than Ivy when Carrie's dad looked at her with a puzzled expression and started laughing. And not just friendly little ha ha's.

"Sorry, we've been worried sick for days. It's not funny. And you should be grounded." His eyes watering, he laughed harder, "Complicated kid stuff. This is really not funny."

He pulled up to her house laughing so hard that tears were running down his cheeks, and the conversation was over. She unbuckled her seatbelt and bolted out of the car, stopping to thank Carrie's dad before shutting the door.

Her dad was already halfway down the stairs and pulled her into a big bear hug.

"Where have you been?"

"Dad. I don't think you'd believe the truth and I'm too tired to make up a lie."

"You can tell us the truth tomorrow. Right now it's bed time for you. No television. No computer or internet games. No phone. No sleepovers. No nothing until the end of the year. And I haven't decided whether I mean the actual year or the school year." His hand was on her shoulder and he squeezed it even while he was telling her of all the ways her life was going to stink for the next several weeks.

"What about Christmas? I wanted a cell phone for Christmas and if I get one, I'll want to use it?" It was never too early to start bargaining with the parents, and besides her parents were softies at Christmas time. They even filled her stocking with chocolate, all the while bemoaning the evils of high fructose corn syrup.

"No cell phone. We already told you that you'll be getting another of the presents on your list."

It was the DAD voice. The great and mighty, the all-knowing, all-powerful firm and final DAD voice. No, Ivy would not be getting a cell phone any time in the next decade, not unless she paid for it herself. Sometimes it was a bother having hippie health-concerned parents who didn't want her to grow up with her nose stuck in a screen. Okay, so Plan A failed. Time for Plan B.

He still had his hand on her shoulder while they walked up the stairs, she decided to pour on the charm and snuggle. It worked a lot better than crying. Then she said, "Daddy" which reminded him of when she was much younger and had the baby cuteness parents couldn't resist, well, except when the babies started screaming, then they weren't so cute. So she started with "Daddy," and then said, "I'm going to be REALLY bored, you know, when I don't have anything to do. Maybe I can use the computer on weekends?"

"Ivy, you'll be lucky if I don't lock you in your room until you're eighteen. I'm too relieved to be angry, but underneath that relief, I'm upset. I don't understand why you snuck out of the house, why you left with Carrie, or how you expect to get away with it without consequences. You are grounded, young lady. And I mean your wings are severely clipped. Feel lucky that I'll let you out of my sight long enough to got to school."

They were through the door and in the front hall. Ivy was ferociously working on Plan C, but for now, she'd settle for a nice hot bath and bed. Suddenly the house seemed empty.

"Where's Mom?"

"Picking up your grandmother. You know she always flies in the night before. I called and let her know you were home. She's been a basket case."

"Wait a minute. Are you telling me tomorrow is Thanksgiving? Is that why all of Carrie's relatives were hanging around?" Ivy stared at her father with shock and dawning horror. No, her father would not let her do anything for a long time. She'd be lucky if she wasn't sitting at the kitchen table with her mother cutting out coupons for the rest of her life.

For his part, her dad was also surprised, "You mean you don't know what day it is?"

"Not really. I mean I knew we were gone a long time, but I kind of lost track. Dad, we didn't just leave town, we left the planet. I don't know where we were, but it was a strange world with dragons and huge birds and people who lived underground."

Ivy told the whole story starting with the egg. Before

she had finished, her mother and grandmother returned even though it was a two hour trip to the airport. Her mother looked terrible. She was pale with huge dark circles under her eyes, and she just kept clinging to Ivy and wouldn't let go.

"Mom, I'm okay."

After an eternity of hugs and tears, Ivy told her story again. She watched her mother and father and then her grandmother and mother exchange glances. The kind that said, *Our daughter/granddaughter has gone crazy or is making this up.* She told the truth even if they wouldn't believe her. She was too exhausted for anything else.

Ivy didn't want to go to bed dirty. She took a long shower, feeling warm and clean as she shampooed her hair. Instead of blow drying her hair, she grabbed a towel and folded it so that her pillow wouldn't get wet. She fell asleep as soon as she curled up under the covers. And this time, she didn't have any strange dreams.

Chapter 18

Carrie's alarm went off at 7:00. She stretched and yawned and started to get ready for school.

"What are you doing up so early?" Her mom stood in the hallway, still dressed in her night shirt and slippers with a hand on the door frame.

"It's already 7:30. We're going to be late." Carrie brushed past her mom.

"Today's Thanksgiving. There is no school. Go back to bed."

With that, her mom left her there in the hall. *Thanksgiving?* She wanted to talk to her mom, but since she'd gotten back her mom was angry, really angry. She'd cleaned the whole house that night, and not just because of Thanksgiving guests. She didn't even ask Carrie how she felt. She didn't care.

Carrie felt a lump in her throat as she puttered back to her room and shut the door silently. Her heart hurt. Didn't anyone care that she had been gone a whole week? Her dad left with hardly a word. Her mom could care less that she returned. Throwing herself on the bed, Carrie wept silently, burying the sound of her crying in the pillow. Things couldn't be worse. Her family was a mess and now she didn't even have Sparky. And it didn't even matter that she existed. Nobody cared.

She could have stayed forever with the underground people and lived like a princess. After she'd cried herself out, Carrie felt a strange awe, not quite peace, more like a shocked exhaustion because she had run out of tears. Not long after that, she fell back to sleep.

The next time she awoke, it was to the smell of warm turkey and the sound of her mother screaming at her father.

"You weren't here. Why is this suddenly *my* fault." Something crashed on the door. That signaled a bad fight. Her mom was throwing breakables. Carrie put the pillow over her head.

"Well, maybe Carrie should live with me. You obviously can't cope taking care of her."

And then her grandmother chimed in, "Now a daughter belongs with her mother. That's the way things are."

Now it was her dad's turn to yell. His voice boomed with anger and even if he wasn't throwing things, Carrie imagined the whole house rattled to the sound of his voice.

"Go ahead and take her. She'll run away from you, too. See if she doesn't." *Mom doesn't want me.* Carrie couldn't get the words out of her head. Go ahead and take her. Go ahead and take her. As if she was a dog or a piece of furniture to be moved around. Maybe she didn't want to go.

Carrie threw back the covers and pushed out of bed. This was the last time she would cower in her room while her parents threw accusations at each other and made everyone's life miserable. This was it. The end. No more hiding under the covers.

Storming down the stairs, Carrie stalked into the kitchen where her father stood by the pantry with his crimson face scowling. Her mom stood by the dishwasher with another plate in shaking hands. The floor in front of the counter near the refrigerator was covered in broken glass. Her mom had thrown it across the room in the general direction of her father, although not close enough to actually hit him.

"She won't run away from me because I won't spend my life in bed." That was pretty low. Carrie cringed when she heard it.

"You left us."

"I left you."

Carrie decided this was as good a time as any to enter the argument. "Actually Dad, you left both of us. I don't recall seeing you much lately, and the times I do you're always in a hurry to be some place else."

"Do you blame me? With treatment like this." He looked ready to storm out again.

"It's Thanksgiving. Aren't either of you thankful for anything?" Carrie would have loved it if they would say *Yes, I'm so glad to have you home again* or *Honey, we love you so much. It's just been a tough year.*

Instead her Mom opened the cupboard and put the plate she was holding away, "Go up to your room. This is between your father and me."

Carrie decided that she was already in so much trouble, one more heaping wouldn't hurt, so she stayed put. "Do you know how many hours I've spent hiding under my covers while you fight? A lot. Send me to Dad's or keep me here. I don't really care. You don't even notice me. You're too busy hating each other."

This was the point where Carrie would normally have

fled the room with tears running down her face, her soul too tender to withstand the same space as her parents after a statement like that. But she didn't leave. She stood her ground. There was a whole new world out there, a place where she was wanted, where princesses acted like they belonged wherever they went.

Her mom frowned, "We don't hate each other."

"It feels a lot like hate to me." Her dad said, "This needs to stop."

"You both need to kiss and make up." Carrie crossed her arms and waited and waited...and waited. The kitchen was silent for a long time, only the sounds of the refrigerator kicking on and the tap tap tap of her mom's fingernails on the counter.

"I'm sorry." Her dad said it. He never apologized, ever.

Her mom cleared her throat and even managed to seem genuine when she asked, "Would you like to stay for Thanksgiving?"

"I wouldn't want to spoil it for you." He bowed his head and took a step into the hall as if he would leave.

"Dad?"

He looked up.

"You won't spoil it for us. Mom's going to be nice today. And you're going to be happy. It will be like a king's court with rules of etiquette and proper conduct. You will speak gently and smile and talk about things like the weather and if the crops will be good this year and how to sew seed pearls and sparkles onto fancy dresses." Carrie lifted her chin the way Minerva did. *Please let this work.*

Her dad moved his cap up and down on his head the way he did sometimes when he was out working on his truck and thinking of a problem. It drove her mom crazy that he wore it in the house. Carrie held her breath.

"Do you want me here?" He was looking at her mom. He didn't ask Carrie. She wanted him. Shouldn't that count for something?

"Yes. If we can just talk about the unimportant things." Her mom attempted a smile. It was pretty lame, but on the whole better than the near-tears anger that she'd had a minute ago.

"I can help with the turkey."

Dad always made the turkey. It was the thing dads did at Thanksgiving. Carrie pleaded with her eyes. But her mom wasn't even looking at her. She was looking at Dad. She still loved him. Carrie knew she did. "That would be nice."

It was the best Thanksgiving Carrie had ever had. Her dad made a joke and her mom laughed and laughed. They were happy, really truly happy. No one asked about where she'd been. It was as if nothing out of the ordinary had happened, except her parents were getting along.

That night, for the first time in weeks, Carrie fell asleep with a smile on her face.

Chapter 19

Monday came all too quickly and soon Ivy was back in class. Ivy asked her mom to drop her off early so that she could talk to Mrs. Huffity. A balding man with huge glasses and a bookish appearance sat at her desk. He leaned over the desk reading an ancient hard cover book. At least it looked ancient to Ivy.

"Where's Mrs. Huffity?"

Startled, the man straightened. "Family leave. She'll be back in a few days."

"Did she say what was wrong?" Ivy asked.

His hand on the spot of the book where he was reading, the new teacher looked more interested in finishing the current chapter than in whether a little dragon had survived her first molting. Scratching his head in that spot where he actually had hair, somewhere between his ear and the top of his head, he said, "I don't pry. Now run along. Class doesn't actually start for a half-hour."

Ivy unpacked her books before heading outside to sit

on the swings and watch for Carrie. The air smelled like frost and wood smoke, and she shivered in the biting cold and waited. Carrie's mom drove up just as the first bell rang. Ivy ran to meet Carrie on the sidewalk.

"You'll never guess. Mrs. Huffity is out today. Family emergency." Ivy grinned, "So are you grounded?"

"No. They didn't even ask where I was. Thanksgiving was so weird. My dad ate dinner with us, and they laughed like nothing had happened."

"That's great! I'm so happy for you." Ivy grabbed her friend's arm and squeezed.

"Don't be. On Saturday they had the biggest fight yet, about a stupid television that sits in the garage. Dad wanted to take it."

"Oh. That stinks."

Carrie bumped the door to the school open a little harder than she needed to. "They didn't even mention that we left. Not once. It's like they didn't even care that I was gone."

"They cared. Maybe they were trying to make Thanksgiving nice for you."

Carrie shook her hair back and shrugged, "Maybe they should have tried a little harder."

Ivy followed Carrie into the classroom, "What about Mrs. Huffity?"

"Maybe she just wanted more time with Sparky." Carrie slid into her seat just as the second bell rang. The substitute wasted no time. While Ivy was outside talking to Carrie, he had written Professor Sheridan on the board.

"Good Morning, Class." He said in that loud voice assembly speakers used when they tried to get kids excited at 8:30 in the morning before anyone should reasonably be excited about anything, except missing class.

Carrie looked over her shoulder at Ivy and whispered in a rather loud voice, "It's way too early for this."

From across the room, Professor Sheridan's rather unwieldy eyebrows knit together furiously and in an equally booming voice said, "What's your name?"

The students had names on the front of their desks. Rather than point that out, she shrugged and said, "Carrie."

"And what exactly did you to say to your friend?"

Carrie could feel the heat warming her cheeks, all the way up to her ears. She hated being called out. "Um...I said that it's too early for this."

Tilting his head, the professor crossed his arms. "Too early for what exactly."

"For you to be expecting us to say *Good Morning*. You'll say *Good Morning class* and we'll say *Good Morning*. And you'll say *I can't hear you* even though we know full well that you can. But you want us to be loud and excited until you want us to be quiet. And seriously most speakers use that bit. It's way overdone. And I'm tired, and I don't really want to say *Good Morning* loud. I don't really know you, and Mrs. Huffity was supposed to start our winter garden today." Carrie took a deep breath and looked somewhat surprised at her own courage before settling back into her seat.

"Go to the principal's office."

Ivy raised her hand, "Mr. Sheridan,"

But he didn't listen. He said, "And while you're at it, take your friend with the glasses with you." Ivy was wearing her backup glasses.

Carrie's eyes widened at the addition of Ivy. That was unfairness in epic proportions. Putting on her best regal princess smile, she nodded once, "I think we shall."

Ivy's mouth hung open and she looked a bit like the time Carrie popped four marshmallows into her mouth all at once just to see if she could. Ivy was more than a little annoyed that she was only known for wearing glasses. That was totally uncalled for.

Carrie could see Ivy was about to say something. She whispered, "Come on. We'll go to the office. Grab your coat."

With a glare at Professor Sheridan, Carrie followed Ivy into the hall. Grabbing her elbow Carrie said, "It's time to use the secret portal magic and go back."

"We're supposed to be going to the principal's office." Ivy said.

"Yeah, but we didn't do anything wrong. You're going to be in trouble anyway when the school calls your parents. And I want to see Sparky." Carrie pulled the bracelet from her jeans' pocket and put it on, grabbing Ivy's hand.

The stones in the bracelet seemed to sparkle in the fluorescent lights. Ivy protested, but Carrie had already activated the portal, and the giant trophy case filled with pottery from the second grade class vanished. "But I don't..."

"want to go back." And suddenly they were in a large obsidian cavern listening to the sound of an animal scream that went further than their ears. Somehow, the sound was in their brain.

Putting her hands over her ears, Carrie said, "Where is this?"

Ivy took off her glasses and wiped her eyes. The screams hurt her heart and she couldn't help but cry.

Chapter 20

The voice was Mrs. Huffity's, that was for sure. "Girls, what do you think you're doing here?"

Ivy groaned and leaned in to whisper to Carrie, "That's the same voice she uses on David."

Carrie looked around the huge cavern, "I know. But where is she? I don't see her anywhere."

When Mrs. Huffity appeared, it was out of a discreet doorway obscured by a rather large boulder. For the first time in Carrie's recollection, Mrs. Huffity was wearing jeans. Her shirt was a huge flowery one, reminiscent of a Hawaiian shirt with large flowers and bright colors.

"Mrs. Huffity, we were worried about you."

It was the eagle eye. Mrs. Huffity had it. Every teacher had it. "Do your parents know you're here? You caused quite a ruckus."

Carrie frowned. It wasn't exactly her fault the first

time. And Ivy said that Mrs. Huffity helped her into this world, so it certainly wasn't Ivy's fault. She pulled her cell phone out of her pocket. "Well, I'll just call my Mom."

"They won't work, Carrie. Nor will texting." Mrs. Huffity's eyes looked large behind her glasses. She leaned in. "Did you come for Sparky? She's looking quite polished with her new scales, but I'm afraid the process is incredibly painful the first time."

"New scales?" Ivy asked.

"Indeed. Come along. You won't likely get the chance to see this again."

Ivy and Carrie followed meekly behind Mrs. Huffity as she led the girls through a twisting and turning hallway, down stairs, through more hallways, up stairs, up more stairs, up more stairs until their legs felt as if they would fall off. And finally, she walked into a large room full of debris.

Sparky caterwauled, rubbing her back and legs against a sharp stone. Large sections of skin flaked off onto the floor.

"How long will it take?" Ivy asked, sending a thought to Sparky *Are you okay?*

Itchy. Sparky's voice hurt Ivy's mind until she felt Mrs. Huffity there, too. And she realized Mrs. Huffity was blocking out much of Sparky's discomfort.

"It's hard for the little ones the first time around. Sparky hasn't had a good molting during this lifetime, but she's coming through it well. Just a few more days..."

Your new scales are beautiful. Carrie said, in awe of the sparkling gold that caught the light and glinted in the cave.

Still itchy. Sparky said.

"Do you want us to scratch your itchy spots?" Carried asked. She was fascinated by Sparky's colorful scales.

If you don't mind. Sparky's voice was considerably more cheerful, and when Carrie and Ivy pet her head, the strange pressure in their heads stopped.

"What just happened, Mrs. Huffity?" Ivy pushed her new glasses back on her nose with one hand while she itched Sparky's neck with the other.

"Sparky missed you both. You know, she impressed on you when she was in the egg. It's rare, and I somehow thought it impossible, but there you have it. She thinks you're her mother, Ivy. And Carrie, you're like an aunt to her." Mrs. Huffity started to cry then, large tears that she swiped from her cheeks.

"What's wrong?" Ivy couldn't help but stare at her teacher, who never seemed unhappy before.

"They grow up so fast, don't they?" She said, her gaze shifting between Ivy and Carrie.

To the girls' surprise, it was Sparky who answered, *Yes, they do.*

They stayed with Sparky for an hour, helping scrub the dead skin from his tail to be replaced with shimmering gold scales that seemed to catch the light. The moment they finished her tail, she stood golden before them and then her ear started to itch and she lifted a leg to scratch the way a dog would use his hind paw, and a fleck of gold fell, leaving an orangish bronze speckle in its place.

"You can't stay here." Mrs. Huffity said, "Carrie, I need the bracelet the underworld princess gave you." She held out her hand the way a teacher confiscating a favorite toy would. The problem was...Carrie didn't want to lose her magical gate.

"Please Mrs. Huffity, in case I want to come back." Carrie couldn't stand the thought of going home, of facing her parents fighting any more. She needed the bracelet. She needed to know she could come back if things got too rough.

"No, Carrie. It would be too easy for you to hide here. And it would hurt your mother to lose both of you at the same time." Mrs. Huffity looked so very wise, and for just that split second Carrie thought she saw a dragon's eyes behind those glasses.

Carrie realized what Mrs. Huffity was saying and her heart sunk, "You mean my dad is really leaving?"

Mrs. Huffity took her glasses off and the sorrow in her eyes was immense. "Carrie, sometimes life doesn't take the direction we want. You have a gift so few have. You know there is more than just the earth. There are so many possibilities and so many people and creatures to love. Don't let this moment of pain destroy you."

Carrie felt pain in her heart. What good was magic if it didn't make a happy ending. "But maybe if you talked to him. I know you're more than you seem."

"We mustn't speak of it, especially when you are home. And my words would make no difference to the situation." Mrs. Huffity put her hand on Carrie's head, much the same way she did Sparky's. "You are delightful, and you have quite the talent for drawing. I'm surprised you haven't taken more time to indulge."

Ivy was listening to the exchange between Carrie and Mrs. Huffity and wondered what drawing had to do with anything. It certainly wouldn't bring Carrie's parents back together.

Carrie smiled quietly, "Thank you."

"Now off you go, before we all get into trouble."

And suddenly, Carrie and Ivy found themselves sitting outside the principal's office. Ivy looked over to see Carrie close her eyes and swallow once.

"Carrie, what she said about your parents...are you okay?"

Carrie shrugged. She didn't know how she felt. "I thought they'd get back together. Mrs. Huffity made it seem so final, you know? Like there's no chance."

Ivy nodded. "That's what I thought, too. But we had an adventure."

"She took my bracelet. Do you think we'll ever have an adventure again? I mean a real adventure?" Carrie kept her voice low because the door opened at just that moment and the secretary walked in.

"We're not even halfway through the school year. And she said she'd be back in a week or so. I'm sure we will."

At that moment, the principal poked his head out of the doorway. "Ah, you're just the two young ladies I want to see."

And that was the end of Carrie and Ivy's adventure

with fierce winds and fiery dragons. Little did they realize when the principal dismissed them that another adventure was just around the corner. After all, there's never a dull moment when your teacher is a fire-breathing dragon...

~ The End ~

40598056R00119

Made in the USA
San Bernardino, CA
23 October 2016